THREE WITNESSES

Borgo Press Books by S. Fowler Wright

Arresting Delia: An Inspector Cleveland Classic Crime Novel

The Attic Murder: An Inspector Combridge & Mr. Jellipot Classic Crime Novel

The Bell Street Murders: An Inspector Combridge & Mr. Jellipot Classic Crime Novel (Prof. Blinkwell #1)

Beyond the Rim: A Lost Race Fantasy

Black Widow: A Classic Crime Novel

The Capone Caper: Mr. Jellipot vs. the King of Crime: A Classic Crime Novel

Crime & Co.: An Inspector Cleveland Classic Crime Novel

Dawn: A Novel of Global Warming

Dead by Saturday: An Inspector Cleveland Classic Crime Novel

Dream; or, The Simian Maid: A Fantasy of Prehistory (Marguerite Cranleigh #1)

Elfwin: An Historical Novel of Anglo-Saxon Times

The End of the Mildew Gang: An Inspector Cauldron Classic Crime Novel (Mildew Gang #3)

Four Callers in Razor Street: An Inspector Combridge & Mr. Jellipot Classic Crime Novel

The Hanging of Constance Hillier: An Inspector Cleveland Classic Crime Novel

The Hidden Tribe: A Lost Race Fantasy

The Jordans Murder: An Inspector Combridge & Mr. Jellipot Classic Crime Novel

The King Against Anne Bickerton: A Classic Crime Novel

The Mildew Gang: An Inspector Cauldron Classic Crime Novel (Mildew Gang #1)

Murder in Bethnal Square: An Inspector Combridge & Mr. Jellipot Classic Crime Novel

The Police and the Public: Some Thoughts on the British System of Justice

Post-Mortem Evidence: An Inspector Combridge & Mr. Jellipot Classic Crime Novel

The Return of the Mildew Gang: An Inspector Cauldron Classic Crime Novel (Mildew Gang #2)

The Rissole Mystery: An Inspector Combridge & Mr. Jellipot Classic Crime Novel

The Screaming Lake: A Lost Race Fantasy

The Secret of the Screen: An Inspector Combridge & Mr. Jellipot Classic Crime Novel (Prof. Blinkwell #2)

Spiders' War: A Novel of the Far Future (Marguerite Cranleigh #3)

Three Witnesses: A Classic Crime Novel

Too Much for Mr. Jellipot: An Inspector Combridge & Mr. Jellipot Classic Crime Novel

The Vengeance of Gwa: A Fantasy of Prehistory (Marguerite Cranleigh #2)

Was Murder Done? A Classic Crime Novel

Who Murdered Reynard? A Classic Crime Novel (Prof. Blinkwell #3)

The Wills of Jane Kanwhistle: An Inspector Combridge & Mr. Jellipot Classic Crime Novel

With Cause Enough?: An Inspector Combridge & Mr. Jellipot Classic Crime Novel

THREE WITNESSES
A CLASSIC CRIME NOVEL

by

S. FOWLER WRIGHT
WRITING AS "SYDNEY FOWLER"

THE BORGO PRESS

An Imprint of Wildside Press LLC

MMIX

CONTENTS

THREE WITNESSES

CHAPTER I.

MR. ROWTON, sole director of Truscott & Rowton, Ltd. (Hydraulic Engineers and Contractors, London and Liverpool), sat at the broad desk of his private office, and looked across at the young man who had come of age only a week before, and who now held a controlling interest in the firm.

Ellis Rowton was a man of fifty, heavily made, with pale intelligent eyes, and a fringe of greyish-yellow hair round the bald expanse of a large head. He had a heavy jaw that had been square once and was fleshy now, but still showed the driving force which had brought him, seventeen years ago, to the place where he now sat.

Roger Truscott, who faced him, was a slim young man of quiet aspect, of whom it was easy to guess that his college triumphs had been achieved in the study rather than upon the field or river. He seemed self-possessed, but may have been more nervous than he allowed himself to appear.

"I would tell you," Ellis Rowton was saying, in the manner of a captain who will not boast overmuch of the storms through which he has steered to a quiet port, "that we have come through some very difficult years. There have been times when I have feared that I might be less than equal to the trust which your father gave me seventeen years ago. But I am glad to say that I have not entirely failed."

"I expect," Roger replied, "that we"—he spoke for his younger brother and himself—"owe you great deal for the ability with which you have carried the business on. I suppose it is doing all right now?"

Mr. Rowton hesitated in his reply. "It is that," he said, "about which I have been anxious to see you. There is, of course, no cause for alarm. We are solvent enough, even so. But the lack of capital, resulting from the losses of earlier years, is a very great embarrassment. Two years ago, we had an offer of amalgamation—in fact, of an outright purchase of the shares in this business—which, in your interest, I should have liked to accept. But I found that there was no power to do so, until you should come of age. With some difficulty, I have kept the offer open. It is not as favourable now as it would have been then. We cannot expect that. But it is still one that I feel we ought to accept. In a word, it would give you and your brother immediate control of £30,000-£15,000 each."

However startled the young man may have been at hearing this proposal on his first visit to the business his father had founded, and of which he now had the right to take at least partial control, he gave little sign of these thoughts.

"You mean," he said, "that there is an offer to buy us all out at five shillings a share?"

"Yes, that's just it."

"And you think it will be wise to accept?"

"Yes. It's a safe way out. We haven't averaged two percent profit in the last ten years, and last year we were a little on the wrong side. Not much, but more than it was healthy to see."

"I suppose we needn't decide at once?"

"Not exactly. The offer's open till the 15th April—that's twelve days from now. After that, it can be withdrawn by notice at any time."

"It doesn't seem long. You see," Roger added, almost apologetically, "it wasn't quite what I expected to hear."

"Well, we're not bound to accept. But I thought I ought to tell you at once. It might have been a good bit worse than it is."

"Yes, I suppose so. Yes, of course. But it's rather a shock at first." He rose up, as though to go.

Mr. Rowton rose also. He said: "If you'd care to have lunch with me, I'll explain how matters stand as well as I can. But, of course, you'll go into them for yourself."

They went out together.

CHAPTER II.

IT was nearly two hours later when they returned. Mr. Rowton entered his office by a private door, explaining as he did so that he preferred that the staff should not always be aware of his periods of absence. "They never know for sure," he said, "whether I'm here or not, unless they knock at the door, and if they do that they've got to have a good reason—and I can see how things are going on in the main office at any time."

He stepped to a small sliding panel, which he drew back, giving a view of more than a dozen clerks seated along a double row of high polished mahogany desks, and of two glass-partitioned offices for the heads of the staff at the further end of the room.

"James," he called out, in a sharp peremptory voice, "I'm ready for the afternoon's mail."

The next moment there was a knock on the door, and a boy entered bringing a wire basket piled with letters. Behind him, a shabby, elderly, thin-nosed man with a slight stoop approached to enter, and then paused.

"Beg pardon, sir," he said, "I didn't know you were engaged."

"This, Menzies, is Mr. Truscott—one of our two largest shareholders. What is it you want now?" And then, as Menzies still hesitated, he added impatiently: "Go ahead, man. We've no secrets here."

"It's about Thornton's cash, sir. There's no doubt of what's been happening. In fact, he's owned up."

A look of annoyance crossed Mr. Rowton's face, and was quickly smoothed away.

"Oh that," he said. "You were quite right to tell me at once. I'm glad he's had the sense to confess. It saves trouble all round."

He turned to Roger Truscott to explain: "It's one of those things that will happen at times in the best managed firms. But it was foolish to try it here. Our system's too good. Just a case of dishonesty on the part of the clerk who has charge of the wages sheets. Not a large amount, I'm thankful to say. A man who's been with us for twenty years, too. One we should have been able to trust. You'd better send him in to me, Menzies. Mr. Truscott is just going."

It was not a remark which Roger had any cause to resent. He had said, ten minutes ago, that he had an engagement for the afternoon, and would only come back to pick up a book he had left. But now he altered his mind.

He had learnt something during the last hour of the man on whose advice he must so largely depend. Perhaps he felt that if he should stay now he would learn more. Perhaps he was attracted by the opportunity of experience in the new drama of life, on the threshold of which he stood. He said: "I don't know that I need go yet. But have him in, all the same. I don't want to hinder you."

Mr. Rowton looked hesitant for a second, and then said: "Oh, of course, if you'd like to stay."

A minute later there was a knock at the door, and a clerk entered of about Menzies' age and figure, and with the same neat shabbiness of attire. He had normally the undistinguished features of a man without imagination or originality: one of those who appear to have been designed by nature for subordinate positions and routine work. It might be postulated with certainty that in all he did he would be accurate, precise, and timid. Dishonesty, in any form, would be an improbable prophecy. Now, as he faced his employer, without apparent observation of the younger man, who had stood somewhat aside near the private door, he had the look of a frightened dog.

Mr. Rowton surveyed him with a cold and contemptuous severity. "Thornton," he said, "you're about the last man I'd have suspected of this. But I'm glad to hear you're making a clean breast of it now. How much have you had?"

"It was £27, sir, but...."

Mr. Rowton, glancing down at a sheet of figures upon his desk, interrupted sharply.

"£27!—that's more than I've got here."

"I'd paid back £4. 3s. 0d. up to last week, sir. If I'd had time—"

"You mean you thought you'd pay it back without anything being found out?"

The smile with which Mr. Rowton asked this question was of an unfriendly derision, but it seemed to give some increase of confidence to the culprit before him. Perhaps it was not going to be so bad after all?

"Yes, sir," he said. "I had hoped to pay it back before any irregularity would be observed. After twenty-two years, sir, and not a shilling wrong all that time. Not a mistake, sir, from year to year. I daresay you can guess how I felt. But if it's not too much to ask that you'll overlook it this once, sir, I'll get it square before Christmas." He looked at his employer's expressionless face, and added eagerly: "I would that, indeed, sir. You can't imagine what a relief it would be. I've hardly slept for the last six weeks."

"Now, Thornton," Mr. Rowton said, with the severity which a man may deserve who demonstrates that, having been a knave already, he must add folly to his offence, "you know it's no use talking like that. You've made your bed, and you've got to lie on it. You've done quite right to confess—though I don't suppose you had much choice about that. I expect Menzies got you too tight—and I don't say we won't ask for a certain measure of leniency when the case comes on; but you know I've a duty to do, a duty to the public and the firm. If I let it be understood that the firm's money was here for everyone to take if they could, and they'd only have to pay it back in the next six months if they got found out—why, you must see for yourself!"

Roger, looking on, saw the flicker of hope go out of the man's eyes, but he was fighting for all that he was and had, for position and home, for wife and children, for the narrow respectability and meagre comforts that might have been his during his remaining years, if a moment's folly (difficult for his own belief) had not thrown him into this pit which threatened ruin, the unmeasured shame of a jail, the shadow of unemployment beyond, and the likely end of a pauper's grave.

"Yes, sir," he said, "I see that. I know how wrong it was, and I can't say how sorry I am. But if you could overlook it just this once. You see, sir, I've been here all my life. I couldn't have thought it possible I should do such a thing myself, and I'd always meant to pay it back. I'm not, sir—I'm not really a thief. If you'd let me tell you just how it happened."

"No, Thornton, I'm afraid I can't. The tale's always about the same, and there's no excuse. And, besides, it's not a matter for me to decide. You can tell all that in the right place and at the right time, and you can be quite sure it'll get heard. I've got a lot to get through this afternoon. I'm bound to give you in charge, and it's no use dragging it out like this. I expect you'll get bail without much trouble. But that's your business. They'll tell you at the station how to go about that."

"Suppose, sir, I could find the money within a—within a week?"

"I'm sorry, Thornton, but it's no use. It's hard on you, of course, but it's a bit late to think about that. It's worse in your position than if you'd been one of the juniors." He touched the bell as he spoke.

Roger interrupted for the first time. "How could you get the money within a week?"

The man was obviously surprised at the question, and the direction from which it came. Till that moment he had not noticed that Roger was there. It had the effect of checking a final outbreak of emotional appeal, which the next second would have brought. He did not know who Roger might be, nor that he could have any power to come to his aid. He saw a young man, plainly not of the business world, very scrupulously dressed and groomed, and wearing the tie of a famous college, whose glance upon him was gravely aloof, as was the tone of his voice. It was not a reasonable supposition that he would have either the will or the power to avert the doom which had just been spoken. But—any port when the storm breaks!

"I could," he began. He had to improvise something, for he had no clear idea of how the money would be raised when he had offered it first. He had been merely fighting for time. "We could sell up the home. It ought to fetch more than that. I'd have done it before, only I daren't let the wife know the trouble I'm in."

"Would that be the only way?"

"Yes, sir. I don't see how else I could find it within a week." (How could he say that he had a wild hope that, when his trouble was known throughout the office, as he had supposed it would be in the next hour, there might be sufficient sympathy to raise the required sum by a subscription among the staff?)

Mr. Rowton had given no attention to this conversation. He had told the boy who answered his summons to ask Mr. Menzies to step in, and that individual, who had not been far distant, was already entering the door.

Roger turned to Mr. Rowton before he could give the instructions he had intended. "Could we have a word about this in private...? If you'd tell them to step outside for a moment?"

Mr. Rowton stared somewhat at this request, at which he was less than pleased. But he had good reasons for wishing to conciliate Roger, and he was too adroit to risk an argument in the presence of his subordinates.

"Menzies," he said curtly, "step outside with Thornton, and wait by the door till I call you back."

The two men went out together, and Roger said, as the door closed upon them: "I hope you won't think that I'm wanting to interfere. But I just wondered whether this was the first time that Thornton's gone wrong."

"The first time? I should say it is! I hope you don't think we keep men on here who have a habit of putting their hands in the till. It's only the second time we've had anything of the kind in the last ten years—and it was a boy then that we'd just put on."

"Then I don't think we ought to let him sell up his home."

It seemed to Roger, vaguely imagining the catastrophe which would suddenly shatter the humble stability of the man's unsuspecting household, that it was an intolerable and needless consequence of a less momentous irregularity, which was already regretted, and, in any event, belonged to the unchangeable past. Why augment the wrong with a further, and quite avoidable, evil?

Mr. Rowton stared in a moment's genuine difficulty of comprehension. "Sell up his home? I don't know that he will. Anyway, he's made his bed, as I pointed out. The more fool he, after all these years, and a safe £6 a week, till he'd have got pensioned off more likely than not. You mean, he'll have a stiff fine? I daresay you're right. They won't jail him, being the first time. Not if he gets a good lawyer to tread on the soft pedal. Of course, there'll be him to pay."

"I didn't mean that. I thought we might drop the idea of prosecuting. But I didn't like the man selling his things to pay the money back all at once. The firm can't be so badly off that it matters that much to us. Anyway, I thought I'd find it myself rather than that."

"It isn't a question of the amount. It's the principle, and the example we have to consider. I think you'd better leave this to me. A man who behaves like that often gets more sympathy than he deserves."

"I daresay he does. He looked rather a rat. But I'd rather pay it for him, if you don't mind, and give him another chance."

"You don't suggest that we should keep him on?"

There was an amazement in Mr. Rowton's voice which caused a doubt to rise in the mind of the younger man. Was he showing himself to be no more than an utter fool? But there was in him a vein of obstinacy, a core of reliance upon his own judgement, beneath his quiet exterior, which would not lightly give way.

"I don't see why not. He wouldn't be foolish enough to do such a thing again, after the fright he's had now. And if you sack him, I don't see how he'd get another job. I shouldn't think it would be easy to do."

Mr. Rowton listened with a rather grim look on an otherwise expressionless face. He cursed inwardly that he should be opposed in the act of public discipline that the occasion required. But he had

15

no intention of quarrelling with Roger Truscott over so indifferent a matter, when there were so much larger issues at stake. He found time to reflect that this exhibition of unpractical altruism might indicate a character which would oppose no difficult opposition to certain plans in his own mind. It was at least sure that Roger Truscott was unsuited to business life!

But it was equally clear to him that it must not be known throughout the staff that he had condoned embezzlement and falsification of accounts.

"Well," he said, "there's only one way to do that. "He went to the door, and called in the two who had stood silently waiting without.

"Menzies," he said, "you did quite rightly to bring this matter to my attention. Thornton had behaved very foolishly in not explaining the way in which he was dealing with the adjustments which have led our auditors, quite naturally, to assume that irregularities were occurring in his accounts, but he may have felt that his length of service with us, and the position of trust which he has held for so many years, exempted him from the necessity of reporting to me, or any possibility of suspicion attaching to himself.

"Thornton," he went on, "while I wish Menzies to understand that I accept your explanation, and that you leave this room completely exonerated, you must realise that you have nothing but your own folly to blame for any annoyance that you have experienced today.

"Menzies, if any rumour of this investigation has spread in the office, I rely upon you to contradict it absolutely. Thornton has the entire confidence of the firm."

Menzies said "Yes, sir," to that. He was a much puzzled man. Thornton, who could have been no less puzzled, had the sense to say nothing at all.

Mr. Rowton added: "You can go now." But as they were racing out he called: "Just a moment, Thornton."

The man stood, when Menzies had gone, in a bewildered uncertainty. He would have broken out next moment into expressions of gratitude, which he yet felt might not be appropriate to the occasion. He could not understand what his fate was intended to be.

Mr. Rowton understood what was going on in his mind, and dealt with the position with the abruptness which he felt it required.

"I don't want to hear anything more from you," he said, in his hardest voice. "Not a word. You will not repay the money. We cannot allow such incidents to be condoned in that way. You will transfer it to the Special Expenses Account. I'll explain to Boddington

16

about that. You'll give no explanation, and say nothing to anyone. If you do, you'll leave in the next hour. And if you want to keep your job from now on, you'll keep straight to the last inch. Now go."

The man did literally as he was told, going without a word.

Mr. Rowton turned to his companion. "Well," he said, with as much geniality as he could bring to his voice, "that's the afternoon's work, and he can think he's a lucky man. By the way, you heard me mention Boddington—he's our auditor. Had that office for ten years past. You might like to see him, and get the firm's position from an independent angle. He'll tell you how he'd value the shares in his own way. I don't want you only to listen to me. You'd better have the address."

He scribbled it on a memorandum pad on his desk, and tore off the slip.

"Thanks," Roger said, "I'll give him a call tomorrow."

He left, feeling some satisfaction in what he had been able to do. He supposed that the way in which Mr. Rowton would have dealt with the dishonesty of a trusted servant was that which most businessmen would approve. Perhaps he owed him some thanks for the readiness with which his own wishes had been allowed to prevail. After all, at the moment he had no claim to override the Managing Director's discretion on such a point. He had the right to claim a seat on the Board (as had his brother also when he should come of age eighteen months later). That right must be exercised within three months, if at all. At present, Mr. Rowton was the sole Director in office. Together, he and his brother could ultimately control the business. They held four-fifths of the shares, the whole voting power of which was now in his hands till his brother should come of age.

But unless, or until, he should claim a seat on the Board, he had no right to interfere in the management of the business, and he saw that some men in Rowton's position might have resented his interposition, which, he was also conscious, there would be many to condemn, as no better in itself than a sentimental folly.

Yet he did not feel any gratitude. He had had his way, but he did not like the method which Mr. Rowton had felt appropriate to the occasion. More seriously, he was disturbed by the proposal that he should sell out of the business, with all the detailed reasons to which he had listened during the luncheon hour.

Yet he saw that it was not reasonable to suppose that his inexperience would be successful in a struggle which appeared to be overpowering all but the most able and resourceful men in the trade—and they with far larger reserves of capital than he could hope to control.

17

But he had spent the last five years in anticipating the day when he would be able to take his father's position in the firm, and in the pursuit of such studies as would fit him therefore. He had had no previous hint of difficulty, or impending disaster. His liberal allowance had always been regularly paid. It was hard for him to adjust his mind so suddenly to a different outlook.

Yet the very proficiency he had gained in the principles of commerce and finance, so far as they can be theoretically learned, had enabled him to understand the explanations which had been given to him far better than he could otherwise have done—better, indeed, than Rowton had supposed that he would be able to do. And they had impressed him in the way that had been designed, for they had been very capably put.

Well, he would see Mr. Boddington tomorrow—and he would delay writing to Cyril till after that.

CHAPTER III.

THE next morning, Roger went to see Mr. Boddington.

The offices of Bagley & Co., Chartered Accountants, of which Mr. Boddington was the sole surviving partner, occupied the upper portion of No. 15, Duckling Street, which is one of those narrow byways, little more than an alley, which are still common in the city precincts.

The building had not been found adaptable for the insertion of a lift in its ancient structure, and Roger climbed three flights of gloomy, circular, wooden stairs before reaching the floor he sought.

The offices which he entered were as drab and shabby as their approach, but it was with a shabbiness too sure of itself to be careful of what it wore. He looked across a stained and battered counter to a room in which four clerks were working, amid a miscellany of desks and tables piled or scattered with papers and books of accounts. He saw files and books stacked in corners and round the walls. He looked up to dusty shelves loaded ceiling-high with accumulations of the same kinds. He saw doors giving entrance to further rooms from which voices came.

A boy took his name, in a brisk, incurious way, telephoned it to his principal's room, and asked Mr. Truscott to take a seat, as Mr. Boddington would see him in a few minutes. Roger sat down beside two other waiting gentlemen, on an ancient bamboo bench which showed projecting horsehair through more than one rent in its leather upholstery.

He took in the details of what he saw with the awareness of one who looks on unfamiliar things. It was all part of a world he had hoped to conquer, which seemed rather more doubtful than it had done when he came to London twenty-four hours before.

He looked at the men beside him. One was uniformed in a style which suggested a bank messenger to his mind, as in fact he was. The other he guessed to be a solicitor's, or perhaps a stockbroker's clerk. His observations were interrupted by the boy's voice: "Mr.

Boddington will see you now, Mr. Truscott." He was led out, along a narrow passage, and shown into a room, the size of which was emphasised by the lowness of its ceiling, and dignified by a dusty carpet, and substantial though dingy furniture.

Mr. Boddington rose from a large desk in the centre of the room as he entered, and came forward a few steps to receive him. He offered the ample comfort of a low upholstered chair, the one luxurious article in the room.

Roger, sinking into its depths, must look somewhat upward at the professional affability of a face that was normally set to the severe cast of mathematics, rather than the romance of life.

"I'm glad," he said, "that you were able to give me a look-in. Mr. Rowton told me that you had come up to town. I expect he's told you also about the offer we have for the shares?"

"Yes, it's about that I came to see you. I want to know whether, as our auditor, you advise the sale, and whether you think the figure's as much as we ought to get."

Mr. Boddington appeared to have no doubt about that. "Yes," he said. "I have advised its acceptance." His tone was one of finality, as though, when his opinion was given, there remained no more to be done than to sign the documents which the deal required.

Observing, however, that Roger did not quickly respond, and supposing correctly that the verdict was not that which he would have preferred to hear, he offered some explanation.

"The offer, speaking between ourselves, is, in my opinion, exceptionally good. It is one which we could not have hoped to obtain, but for a convergence of business interests, which is not likely to recur. The fact is that the business, at the moment, would be of far greater value to the purchasing syndicate than it can possibly be in its present hands. The sale would eliminate competition, and the business would pass into the control of those who have ample capital to exploit it properly."

"But I suppose a year or two of good trade would make the shares worth a much higher figure?"

Mr. Boddington shook his head slightly. "A year or two? A much higher figure? Scarcely that. A somewhat higher, no doubt. But, I must tell you, that is an improbable eventuality. There is a more likely—and perhaps I should say a more sinister—contingency to which I must draw your attention. It is a responsibility which falls upon me, in view of your inexperience of business matters. The value of the ordinary shares in a commercial undertaking is always precarious. It may be (as it is here) dependent entirely upon the business continuing. If it were closed tomorrow, the claims of creditors, of bankers and mortgagees, would swamp the assets. I can assure you that you would get nothing at all.

"At the present moment, it would take no more than a short period of adverse trading, a slight fluctuation in market conditions, to render your shares of no realisable value whatever. No, Mr. Truscott," he concluded, in the voice of one who has shown a sufficient patience with the hesitation of ignorance, and assumes the acceptance of the advice he has given, "I can assure you that the offer is not one to be put aside. Indeed, I should have been obliged to advise its acceptance, had it been for a less amount, or offered in a less liquid form."

He sought among the papers that piled his desk. "I have here the document which the solicitors sent over this morning. You will see that it is brief but simple, but, as a matter of form, I should like you to read it over before you sign it. You will observe that it covers your brother's interest as well as your own, and provides for an immediate cash payment of £30,000, half of which you would, of course, hold in trust for him.

"You may like to know that it will be paid to you without deduction—I shall be able to obtain a certified cheque made out to yourself in exchange for this document—as it is a condition that all expenses incidental to the transaction shall be the liability of the purchasers.

"Miss Morton, I shall want you to witness this gentleman's signature."

As he concluded, Roger, following his eyes, became fully aware for the first time of a third occupant of the room, a girl who had been seated at a small table in the dimmest corner, and who now rose and came forward.

"I'm afraid," he said, with a diffidence of manner which did less than justice to the resolution of his own mind, "I'm not prepared to decide anything just yet. I want to think it over a bit more."

He was not insensible to the force or gravity of the arguments which had been put before him, but he had an instinctive objection to being rushed. He had entered that office to enquire, not to decide, supposing that the company's auditor would give impartial advice. Well, such it might be. But, all the same he would sign nothing today.

As he had spoken, Mr. Boddington had already risen, to offer him the use of his own chair in executing the document. Now he looked at him with the controlled impatience which may be shown to a child's folly, perhaps excusable in itself, but exasperating in its results.

21

"It is, of course, of little moment to me," he said. "The loss is yours. But I am bound to advise you that, if you let this opportunity slip, you will be guilty of an almost incredible folly."

"I am not sure," Roger said, "that it is what my father would have liked me to do."

"Your father," the accountant replied, with an amount of reason which Roger was obliged to recognise, "showed the extent of his confidence in Mr. Rowton by the position in which he placed him. It is no more than a logical deduction that he would have wished you to take his advice on a matter which you should recognise that he is much more competent to decide."

"Yes," he replied frankly, "I see that. But it was my father's intention, as it is stated in his will, that the arrangement he made should conserve the business for his sons to follow. It could not have been his wish that we should sell out the first moment that we have the power."

"But he could not foresee the business conditions that now prevail."

"It would be a less responsibility if I were deciding for myself only, but I am asked to sell my brother's shares also."

"That is the very point, Mr. Truscott, which I was about to bring to your notice. If you refuse this offer, your brother, when he will come of age in about eighteen months, may succeed to nothing better than shares which have become unmarketable. You may have deprived him of his entire fortune if you refuse this offer, against the judgement of those who are most competent to advise you."

Roger had realised this already, and it was not a risk he could take lightly. He asked: "I suppose we can't sell part, and hold part?"

His thought was that he would sell half if he could, giving his brother the ultimate benefit of whichever might prove to be the more profitable policy. But the idea proved to be impracticable.

"Obviously not," Mr. Boddington replied, with a shortness of tone implying that Roger's objections and difficulties were approaching perversity, "the offer is to buy out the firm for purposes of amalgamation."

Though with a stubborn reluctance, Roger was near to yield at that moment. But he remembered that there was one question he had not raised, which had been on his mind during the night. It was one that he felt some diffidence in putting, but he had a quiet persistence of character which did not lack courage, and the reminder that he had his brother's interests, as well as his own, to guard strengthened his resolution. After all, it was a point on which he was entitled to be fully informed.

22

"I suppose—I mean, I think I ought to know—does this sale involve Mr. Rowton's retirement, or will he retain his position?"

It was a question which caused the accountant to look at Roger with a new keenness, as though weighing him afresh; but he showed no indisposition to answer it. "Mr. Rowton will take a place on the Board of the purchasing company. Had he not consented to that, it would have been impossible to secure you so favourable an offer—if any at all. I suppose, Mr. Truscott, you cannot be expected to realise how much, in the course of years, the goodwill of the firm has become inseparable from Mr. Rowton himself, or what its position would be if he should have decided to withdraw himself from it. Do you suppose that your shares would have any value then?"

"I don't know how that would be. I didn't mean to suggest anything. I only thought that it was a point on which I should be informed. But I should have supposed that the terms of Mr. Rowton's appointment with us would have rendered it impossible for him to act in opposition under any circumstances."

"Well, so they may. I can't say about that. I wasn't suggesting that he ever had such a thought in his mind. I only wished you to realise what his position is, and how much reason you may have for gratitude that he has brought matters to a point at which you can pick up so large a fortune. If you are satisfied now, perhaps you will sign the deed?"

"I think I should like to think it over—at any rate for a couple of days."

Mr. Boddington recognised defeat, for that occasion at least

"I suggest," he said, "that you should use that time to consult your brother. You may find him to be of a different mind."

Roger said: "Yes, I will do that."

He thought there could be little doubt as to what Cyril would say. He would take the cash with both hands, if he had his choice. To ask him, and then to decline to sell, would throw the maximum responsibility upon himself, if his decision should prove disastrous in the end.

Still, it ought to be done.

He rose to go.

Miss Morton, who had stood waiting while this conversation proceeded, went back to her chair.

Mr. Boddington shook hands, with no warmth of cordiality, but with no more show of annoyance than was natural in one whose opinion had been too lightly regarded. "Well, think it over," he said, "and don't be too quick to refuse the advice of those who know how the land lies."

Roger went out, and entered a nearby restaurant of frugal respectability, where he ordered lunch. A few minutes later, a young lady hesitated and then sat down opposite to him. The tables had been filling up since he came in, and seats were few.

He glanced at her and observed a face that he had seen half an hour before, being that of Miss Morton, Mr. Boddington's secretary. It was one at which any man might be glad to look twice.

He had a correct impression that when he was not looking at her, she was observant of him. He repaid her in the same way. More than once, by this process, their glances met and withdrew. But, beyond that, shyness held them apart. They both lingered somewhat over the meal. In the end, Miss Morton, having less liberty of time, was the first to go.

CHAPTER IV.

"Of course, we'll take the cash," Cyril said, with some impatience at his brother's hesitation. "We should be mugs if we didn't. Fifteen thousand isn't to be sneezed at these days, and I don't reckon it ever was. And you say yourself that everyone tells you it's a good get-out."

"Not quite everyone. Look at this." Roger handed his brother a strip of paper, such as might have been torn from a cheap writing-pad, on which was written in block capitals,

IF YOU'RE WISE YOU WON'T

The two brothers were standing in the window of the lounge of the Ridgway Hotel, in which Cyril had engaged a room for the night, having come up to town on Roger's suggestion to discuss the proposed deal.

Cyril, though the younger, was some inches the taller, and much the heavier of the two. He was more proficient in sports than studies, and pulled stroke in the University boat. His sporting activities had the beneficial effect of keeping him sober for long periods, when he was in training for any competitive event, which was not his invariable condition. Now he turned the strip of paper over, looking for a signature that was not there.

"Where did you get this? Who is it from?"

"I don't know. Rowton's found me a room where they bring me accounts and correspondence to look at. I'm supposed to be studying the state of the business. Of course, they bring me what they're told. I found this on the table, when I got back from lunch yesterday."

"You might have asked who'd been in while you were away."

"So I might, and perhaps got some poor beggar sacked for nothing worse than trying to give me the straight tip. I thought it best to say nothing."

"But it mayn't be that at all. It's someone trying to queer the pitch, but you can't tell why. He may think he'll lose his job if the amalgamation comes off. There's one safe bet, that when he wrote that he was thinking of his own skin rather than ours. Anyway, you wouldn't take more notice of a thing like that than of the opinions of men who gave us reasons, and know how to sign their names."

"No, I don't say that I should. But I'm not easy about the whole thing. I don't like Rowton, and though he tries not to show it, I feel he's too eager to get me to fall in."

"Well, that's natural enough, if he thinks it's a good deal. We're all in the same boat. You mayn't like him, but you've only seen him about three days. Father must have known him better than you. How soon can we touch the cash?"

"They'll pay it over anytime if I sign. I suppose that means that they've got all the other signatures that they need, and I'm the one that's holding it up. I wish I didn't feel so reluctant to do it."

"And how long can you hold them off?"

"It's about a week now before the offer could be withdrawn."

"Well, don't dally too long." He looked at Roger's doubtful irresponsive face, and a sudden fear came into his own. "You wouldn't really—" he exclaimed, as though the almost incredible folly had only just entered his mind as a serious possibility. "You wouldn't really let this money go loose?"

"No. I don't promise, but I expect I shall accept. There doesn't seem much else to be done."

"No, I should think not! If I thought—" Cyril broke off the sentence, leaving the threat which underlay the new truculence in his tone to his brother's imagination. He added, as another thought came to disturb his mind: "And you won't play the elder brother with me, or I'll know why. I don't want any Trusteeship business, or 'wait till you're twenty-one.' I'll come up on Thursday next, and I'll look to you to have the cash ready by then. I suppose there'll be no legal reason for holding it back?"

"No. I think not. I suppose I'm responsible, and could hold it till you're of age, or pay it over at once. But I don't know why I shouldn't do that. I expect you'd blue it in about the same way then as now."

"I'm going to have a good time with it, if you mean that. But you're a long way out, if you think I shall just chuck it away. Going now? So long. I'll get leave to come up on Wednesday again, and I'll trust you to shell out then."

Roger, walking away, felt that, whether his instinct of reluctance were right or wrong, the issue must be the same. He was caught in a current against which he might strive, but could not hope to prevail.

For, as Cyril had talked and blustered, he had looked ahead, and seen that, if he should have his own way at this time, and should prove so far right that the business would be carried on successfully for the next eighteen months, yet he would be steering to an almost certain wreck at that time.

At present he could claim a director's place, giving him equal power with Mr. Rowton, though the absence of the same detailed knowledge and experience of the business might make its practical exercise difficult. He had a further power, in that he could convene a shareholders' meeting on any serious issue, when he could vote down all opposition. But that would only be during his brother's minority. In eighteen months, if the shares were still held, half of them would pass to him, with their voting power. Cyril could claim an equal seat on the Board. Or he could sell the shares to whom he would.

To have power for eighteen months would be of little use, if it must entail making enemies on all sides, who could contrive to thwart him at last.

He saw that Cyril would be hostile and embittered, if he should refuse to make the instant sale which would put into his hands the money on which he counted already with eager greed. Even if his obstinacy should be so far justified that the business would be prosperous, and the shares saleable eighteen months hence, his brother's most likely action would be to sell them to anyone who would be willing and able to buy, as he himself would be powerless to do. And anyone who should purchase his brother's shares could make a combination against him which would render his own votes impotent. To engineer such a position, Cyril's shares might be worth almost as much as were the whole quantity which he now controlled. He might find that he had done no more than to fill Cyril's pocket, while his own would be left half-empty.

They might even be able to combine to throw him off the Board. There were legal questions on which he was far from clear, and not sure of where he could get sound and impartial advice. But he had wondered whether, at the worst, he could not turn Rowton out with the votes he had, if it should prove impossible to work together, and what is sauce for the goose.... It might depend upon agreements he had not seen. He supposed he ought to go to the Company's solicitors. So he had been invited to do. And so he would. But he must do it with a sense of uncertainty as to whether everything he said might not be reported to Mr. Rowton, as soon as he should walk out of the door. He felt, with some bitterness, that his youth and inexperience of business life were a handicap too great to be overcome. The advice he heard from all sides might be disinterested or not (and it was rather difficult to formulate his doubt to a logical probability), but he saw that all around him were of one mind, and it might be beyond his strength to resist, even had he been more than sure that it was the right course to take.

If Cyril had been of a kindred spirit, the two together might— and yet, perhaps, even then.

He walked on in a gloomy doubt, only relieved by another purpose that caused him to loiter the way he went, for a destination at which he did not wish to arrive too soon; and meanwhile Mr. Boddington, having called up Mr. Rowton on the phone, was saying: "Is that young fool going to sign? Well, he *must*. And there mustn't be much delay about it either. Yes, it's sure. I've just had a code cable. 'Enter.' Yes, that's the word. Well, I needn't say any more. I leave it to you."

Miss Morton, who had paused in the typing of a report, so that the conversation should not be disturbed by the noise of the instrument, heard this end of the conversation, but Mr. Boddington was not concerned about that. Even if she were interested, or understood it, which he had no reason to suppose, he knew that she was not one to betray the confidence of her employer. He chose his staff with discretion, and often for very different qualities from his own, and he had found that it paid him to pay them well.

So, having concluded this conversation to his satisfaction, he went out to lunch. A few minutes later, Miss Morton did the same; and a few minutes later still, Roger Truscott, having loitered long enough to make it reasonably certain that she would have settled herself in what he rightly supposed to be her usual midday resort, entered by the same door, looked round in as casual a manner as his eagerness would allow, and took a seat at her table.

CHAPTER V.

ROGER TRUSCOTT had something more than the average shyness of a sisterless youth, who has been of too fastidious a habit to mix much with the more outspoken members of his own sex, or the bolder ones of the other, and whose knowledge of life has been most largely gained from the printed page.

But this shyness was controlled by a spirit which would not fail to provide whatever courage might be required for the occasion it had to meet. What he had resolved, he would do. Twice before—once by chance, and once by his own design—he had sat opposite Diana Morton, in a silence which he would have been glad to break, but in which his eyes only had spoken; and, in the intervals, the memory had distracted him continually from the surely more urgent question of whether he should sign a deed which would produce fifteen thousand pounds to his immediate possession.

He saw that, if he should find her table again, it must be of an unmistakable significance, and he told himself that it would be no less than unmannerly impertinence if he should do so without ascertaining that his conduct was not resented. He might even merit, and receive, a word of sarcastic or indignant protest, such as would double-bolt the door which he was seeking to open.

Reflecting thus, he had resolved upon a line of attack which he thought it would be difficult to resent, and which, without the formality of introduction, would still be natural in view of the place and circumstances in which they had met.

After a few minutes, occupied on his side in some uncertainty as to how she might be regarding his appearance at the same table as herself on a third occasion, to resolve which he had nothing to guide him beyond the fact that she gave no sign of observing his presence, he determined to test the wisdom of the method of assault which had seemed so simple, indeed so obvious, when it had occurred to him during the night.

He was to ask the question in a casual, natural way, the first time that he should happen to meet her glance, and, after that, conversation would easily develop. The first difficulty he experienced was that the glances which had been freely directed upon him on the first occasion, and more frugally on the second, were now entirely withheld. He was too ignorant of the facile theories which explain all women alike to attempt interpretation of this withdrawal, but he felt that it gave an added formality to the question which he had resolved to ask, though he would not let it deter him.

"Excuse me, Miss Morton, but could you tell me whether Mr. Boddington would be in this afternoon at about three, if I should look in at that time?"

He was aware, as he spoke, that the question, carefully phrased in his mind before he commenced, had no genuine sound. The girl lifted her eyes to regard him silently, her brows meeting in a puzzled frown.

"I don't make appointments for Mr. Boddington," she said, after a pause that seemed to Roger much longer than it actually was. "It might be best to telephone first."

"I beg your pardon," he said awkwardly. "I thought you might happen to know."

She made no answer to this, and the stubborn core of his own nature caused him to continue the conversation on the lines which he had planned already.

"The fact is I'm not sure whether I ought to see Mr. Boddington, or the firm's solicitors, Tonks & Weatherhead. You see, I don't know much about the etiquette of these matters. I've only been up in London a few days, and I don't know anyone here. I suppose they are a reliable firm?"

He got an answer at last. She looked at him again in a cool way, and said: "Quite." As she did so, she rose, leaving the table at an earlier time, and after a shorter meal than her habit was, as he had observed it on the two previous occasions.

He was left with a consciousness of defeat, and a suspicion that it might have been his own fault. He had wanted to talk to the girl, and his mind had been occupied, at the same time, with doubts and suspicions regarding the men who had his business interests in their hands; and the two motives had converged to produce those awkward queries which had been so coolly rebuffed. His desire to know more of Messrs. Tonks & Weatherhead had been real enough. Vaguely he had thought that in conversation with her he might learn something which would assist him to the decision which he found so difficult. It had been an end in itself, though it might have been considered first as a means to another. But it had proved to be no more than a double blunder.

Well, he must find some other method by which to know her, to break through her reserve. After all, her tone had been no worse than noncommittal and cool. It had been free from any indication of hostility or resentment. He was not of the disposition to withdraw from a first defeat. Curiously and illogically, this repulse increased his indisposition to give way on the quite separate business issue which also engaged his mind.

He went back to Cannon Street to the Truscott & Rowton offices, where he was to be occupied in the inspection of elaborately tabulated records of the specifications to which the firm had estimated during the last three years (from which he was intended to learn that they could only obtain contracts by quoting prices which were unremunerative to them, though they might be profitable to their better equipped competitors). He felt less depressed than he might have been expected to do. He might have realised his position in a worse light had he heard the conversation which took place between Diana Morton and her employer when he came in from lunch that afternoon. Mr. Boddington had listened to a few words from one of his staff as he passed through the outer office, and there was a frown still on his face as he asked the girl: "Anything happened since I went out?"

"Only Mr. Clifford's rung up to know whether you can attend the Restall meeting for them next Wednesday. It's 4:00 P.M. I told them yes, as far as I knew, but I would let them know definitely when I'd spoken to you. And Mr. Truscott saw me at lunch, and asked if you would be in at three."

"Is he coming in?"

"I couldn't say, but I don't think he really wanted to know. I think he was trying to find out whether he could get any information from me, so I cut him short. I'd like to know what you wish me to do if he tries again."

"What information did he try to get?"

"It hardly went that far. He asked about Tonks & Weatherhead—were they a good firm? And I said yes, of course. But I didn't know what you'd wish me to say if he went on, so I didn't let him. He came and sat opposite to me at lunch yesterday, but he didn't try to talk till today."

Mr. Boddington considered this. It confirmed the report that he had had three minutes before from a clerk who had been sitting no more than four tables away. It also confirmed his previous judgement that Miss Morton was a reliable secretary. But there is no wisdom in trusting anyone more than you are obliged to do.

He said: "You'd better tell him that you know nothing. But let him talk as much as he likes, and let me know what he says. If the young fool can't understand when he's well off, he'll end up with nothing, more likely than not." (She could tell him that, if she would.)

He thought that Roger Truscott was a troublesome young cub, and more pertinacious than was indicated by his mild exterior. But Rowton could be trusted to deal with him.

CHAPTER VI.

It was on the following Monday, the 10th of April, toward the end of the afternoon, that Mr. Boddington was informed that Mr. Rowton was coming to see him, and would be over in twenty minutes.

Shortly after that, Mr. Boddington asked Miss Morton to complete a letter of some importance, and added that the remainder of the correspondence could be left till the next day. He said that she could leave a bit early for once, which she was pleased to do. When Mr. Rowton arrived, and was shown into Mr. Boddington's room, he found that gentleman alone. Without the formality of shaking hands, he rose and closed a felt-lined door which doubled that by which his visitor entered.

Mr. Rowton observed, as the key turned: "I see you guess why I have come."

"I know he hasn't been here to sign; and it's a week now since he came to town."

"Well, I've done all I could."

"Then you've got to do a bit more."

"It's no use. He's made up his mind he won't. He's like a mule, for all his quiet ways."

"Nonsense! A boy like that, with no advice, and knowing nothing of business matters, except what he's read in books. Rowton, you're enough to make a man sick. Do you mean he's told you he won't?"

"Not in words. But he's made it clear enough. He gets more determined every hour. He told me this morning that he couldn't see why we shouldn't pull the business round, and get the shares back to par, and he was sure that was what his father would have wished him to do. But there's more than that. He wrote to his brother this afternoon. Dictated it to one of the girls, who read it back to me when I had her in. The letter says there's no need for his brother to come up on Wednesday, as he's decided to hold on to the shares, and take a seat on the Board. He's been at the books all the time since he came up. I shouldn't have thought it possible he'd learn so much in the time."

"He can't learn anything from the books that he shouldn't know."

"I don't say he can, in the way you mean, but he's learned a damned lot more than we want him to. He's been with T. & W. a good bit too, and got some things from them."

"Weatherhead would advise him to sell."

"So he would have done at the first, and I don't say he doesn't now. But I'd give something to know all that's gone on in that office."

"I don't suppose you'd hear much if you did. You'd be a better man if you didn't funk at things you can't see. But it's your part to do this, and you're going to see it through. You'll have the fellow here before five tomorrow, with his pen in his hand, or we'll talk again in a different way."

Mr. Rowton's face flushed angrily. But he made no protest against the insulting words, or the vague menace of their conclusion. His eyes fell before the cold anger and contempt of those that were fixed upon him.

"You know," he said, "I'll do what I can. It's as much to me as to you."

"It's all that, and a lot more," was the curt reply.

Mr. Rowton went, without further words.

CHAPTER VII.

DIANA MORTON was loyal to her employer. Mr. Boddington had been correct in that assumption, as he most often was. If she saw and heard things in his offices which were beneath her own code, she supposed them to be no worse than were generally permitted by the lower ethics of business life. She could not reasonably hold herself responsible for the contents of the letters she typed, or the accuracy of the accounts that she duplicated. In her work she was quiet, exact, efficient. She was paid a liberal salary, which she fully earned. Her business experience, after the completion of her secretarial training, had begun in that office, so that she had observed no other standards with which to compare it.

So far, Mr. Boddington could have diagnosed her with as much accuracy as she knew herself, and something more beyond that. But there was one point on which he would have been widely wrong. He underestimated the activity of her intelligence; he did not guess how much of growing knowledge and understanding her silence held.

When he engaged her, he had recognised her qualities of character as acutely, and chosen her for them as definitely as for those of education and secretarial proficiency. He would have seen no more force in the criticism that he did not cultivate such qualities in his own character, than a ship's captain would feel if he were told that the ship's cook would make a better omelette than himself. He navigated the business of Bagley & Co., and selected his staff for the various qualifications of brain or character that their positions required.

The mistake he made was that which is common among clever and unscrupulous men of linking rectitude with obtuseness, if not actual stupidity, as its complementary quality.

He would have been very greatly surprised had he been made aware of how clearly Miss Morton understood, from casual hints, and half-heard telephone conversations, the nature and extent of the plot which had been woven to deprive the Truscott brothers of their rightful heritage. But she did not regard it as a matter in which she had any personal part, nor did it arouse any active interest in her mind until the day when she was led by a fateful chance to seat herself at a table with Roger Truscott, and to become conscious, with the swift instinct of femininity, that he was not unaware of, or indifferent, to her.

When he found her table on the second day, she did not fail to interpret his action correctly, as being in deliberate pursuit of her own attractions, nor was the secret thrill of excitement that a girl may feel when she is first conscious of such pursuit deadened by any instinct of antipathy, or, more fatal, indifference, to the man whose attention had been drawn toward her.

There might have been no other sequel than the age-old idyll of youth and love, had not Roger addressed her with those sudden blundering questions, and had she not been conscious for some previous minutes that Teddy Watts was only four tables away.

She knew Teddy well enough to guess with instant accuracy the interpretation which he would be likely to place upon the fact that she was lunching with Roger Truscott, and that he would report it when he got back to the office.

With this realisation, there had risen the unwelcome doubt— suppose that Teddy's idea should be partly true? Suppose that. Mr. Truscott was really seeking her acquaintance, not for herself, but in the hope that he could extract some business information from her?

While she doubted thus, she was roused, and her doubt confirmed, by Roger's fatuous question. How she would have answered under other circumstances, and to what confidences it might have led, can be no more than a vain conjecture. She might even then have refused to discuss matters on which it is at least certain that she would not consciously have betrayed her employer.

But with the knowledge that Teddy was looking on, and the subconscious realisation (which was almost a conscious pain) that Roger Truscott's interest in herself might be quite impersonal, the manner of her rebuff was a natural sequence.

The same two reasons united in the same conscious and subconscious way to suggest that she should report to Mr. Boddington that Roger had approached her thus; but, having done this, her mind was led to dwell upon the whole affair with a more personal interest than she was accustomed to give to Mr. Boddington's business enterprises.

She saw the full singularity of the fact that it should rouse some suspicion in any mind that one of the clients of the firm should cultivate friendship with her, and she was led to a sharper realisation of the moral standards prevailing in the offices where she had gained her sole experience of professional usage. She felt that there must be others, practising a different etiquette and a higher morality, but she had the feminine characteristic of being more strongly influenced by the particular than the general; and, when the thought of resignation came to her mind, it was impulsed rather by the fact that she was witness of an unscrupulous intrigue in which her sympathies had passed over to the opposite camp, than by any moral recoil from the abstract principles of the firm she served.

A desire to warn Roger Truscott against a plot of which she was now clearly aware, and which aimed to rob him and his brother of the main part of their inheritance, might or might not have been sufficiently strong to lead her to resign the comfortable position she held, had she not felt a scruple of honour as to whether she would even then have been free to disclose that which she had already learnt; and this hesitation was strengthened by the reflection that Roger Truscott, for all she knew, might be sufficient for his own protection. He might not require her aid. She might resign a most comfortable position to no purpose, and receive no thanks.

These doubts and hesitations occupied her during the hours while the deed lay awaiting Roger's signature on Mr. Boddington's desk, and he did not come; and while she heard Mr. Rowton being summoned to another conference, which was to take place that evening after she had left the office. But they were forgotten with the news of the tragedy of the following day.

Wednesday opened in Bagley & Co's offices with the usual routine business, in which Mr. Boddington became engrossed, having seemingly put the affairs of Truscott & Rowton, Ltd., for the moment, out of his mind. Miss Morton's curiosity as to what might be the issue of last night's conference remained ungratified until he made some clearances of his desk before leaving for lunch. Then he came on the unsigned deed, and passed it over to her, remarking: "You'd better file this. I understand that Roger Truscott has definitely refused to sign, and that blocks the whole deal. Remind me, if necessary, to give you letters to close it tomorrow morning. There'll be some papers to send back to Mr. Weatherhead. I shall be away at Thompson's meeting this afternoon."

She supposed that Roger had won, without the need of any information from her, which it would have been treacherous to supply (she saw that clearly now), even though she had resigned before doing so. She was not surprised that Mr. Boddington showed no concern at this issue, for it was not his habit to be outwardly ruffed by the loss or gain of a business coup, nor was she supposed to be aware of the inwardness of the matter.

Still, she did know. She knew not only the largeness of the stake, but of other financial facts which had made it a matter of critical urgency that it should be won. She must wonder still what the end would be.

She went quickly on with her work during the afternoon, until the time came when Stubbs entered with the usual tea tray. His eyes were round with excitement.

"Ow, miss," he said happily, "ain't it 'orrible?"

"What's the matter now?" she asked, without supposing that he had anything of much interest to communicate, for she knew Dick.

"'Aven't you 'eard, miss?" He was stirred to wonder that anyone could be isolated from an event of such moment. "Not about the murder at Rowton's? Not about Mr. Truscott's murder? Shot, he was, and then fell down the stairs. It's in the papers this afternoon."

Diana's familiarity with a quality of imagination in Stubbs's composition, which rendered a discount of eighty percent no more than a conservative deduction from any statement for which he might be responsible, helped her to receive this news with an aspect of outward serenity; but she found some difficulty in controlling her voice to its normal tone, as she answered: "All in the papers, is it? Then suppose you run out and get me one, and I'll read it while I have tea."

Dick took the offered penny and disappeared, but his return was so instant as to make it clear that the paper he brought had been already circulating in the outer office.

She waited until he had left the room before opening it, to read, in heavy block capitals across its front page:

TRAGEDY IN CITY OFFICE
UNIVERSITY BLUE SHOT DEAD

She read the few leaded lines below, which must be followed to an inner page before it became definite that it was not Roger Truscott, but a brother of whom she had heard but had not seen, whose life was so abruptly terminated:

Shortly after 1:00 P.M. today the police were summoned to the Cannon Street Offices of Truscott & Rowton Ltd., where they were shown the body of a young man lying at the foot of a flight of stone stairs, which lead from the private offices to a side entrance in Filkin Street. The body, in which life was extinct, has been identified as that of Mr. Cyril Truscott, younger son of the founder of the firm.

Mr. Truscott had been shot, apparently by a revolver which was found lying upon the stairs, but it is uncertain whether death was due to this cause, or to the injuries which he received in his fall.

Mr. Truscott was a member of the Oxford boat-crew, and a well known golfer.

That was all the detail obtainable from a paper which must have gone to press within two hours of the time when the police were first informed of the tragedy; except that, in the stop-press column, there was a further brief announcement:

In connection with the death of Mr. Cyril Truscott, his brother, Mr. Roger Truscott, was interviewed by Inspector Byfleet at about 2:00 P.M. at the Royalty Restaurant, where he was lunching. After a short conversation he was invited to accompany the Inspector to Scotland Yard, where he is stated to have been detained.

Miss Morton saw clearly enough that the question of selling or holding shares might be of little more remaining interest to the living brother than to the dead. If it were really so...it was hard to believe. And yet she knew that, in such matters, the metropolitan police do not make many mistakes. And Roger Truscott was detained on account of his brother's death. And there would be the lawyers to pay. "Yes," she said to herself, "I suppose he will sell now."

She saw that Mr. Boddington was likely to have his own way once again, as he mostly did.

CHAPTER VIII.

The morning newspapers contained the definite announcement that Mr. Roger Truscott had been arrested, and charged with his brother's murder; the afternoon ones, that he had appeared before the magistrate, and been remanded for seven days at the request of the police. He had looked pale but composed. Mr. Leslie Tonks (Tonks & Weatherhead) had appeared for the prisoner.

When asked if he had any objection to a remand, the solicitor had had a few whispered words with his client, after which he had replied that he must consent to the remand, but he was instructed to say that the prisoner absolutely repudiated the charge, and denied all knowledge of his brother's death. The whole proceedings lasted less than five minutes.

Those who were present in court could have added some details which editorial discretion declined to publish. It had been clear from the reporters' table that the whispered exchanges between the prisoner and his legal representatives had not been of a harmonious character, and it appeared evident that the statement the solicitor had made, denying all knowledge of the crime, had been against his own judgement and instruction. The prisoner's final words: "Then if you don't say it, I shall," had come clearly to the reporters' table, after which Mr. Leslie Tonks had risen and made the declaration of innocence which his client claimed.

The afternoon papers contained a variety of other details, concerning both the accused and the murdered man, and the scene and circumstances of the tragedy, but they were restrained by the rule which forbids comment upon any event after it has become the subject of a criminal charge, and while the legal process continues; and there is more to be gained from the discussion which proceeded in the offices of Messrs. Tonks & Weatherhead, when Mr. Leslie Tonks returned from court, and reported the circumstances of the case to his senior partner.

Leslie Tonks was depressed. A young man of normally optimistic temperament, and of a romanticism somewhat unusual in his profession, he had been disposed to think that the great occasion would not find him unequal to it. The great occasion had come. The case in which he was appearing would be reported as widely as the English language is spoken, and in a few additional countries. He would be unable to show his legal abilities at the trial itself, for which counsel must be briefed, but the magisterial enquiry which precedes the trial is often no less than a full-dress rehearsal, at which the grounds of attack and defence are chosen, and the final battle may be lost or won. So far, he could take control, and it was a position such as an able lawyer may often find sufficient to establish a lifelong reputation in the criminal courts.

But now he paced the room as he talked, in an excitement of irritation. He said bitterly: "He gives us no chance at all."

Mr. Weatherhead sat by the fire, for the morning was chilly, and he was an old man, no longer in robust health. He listened with a sad gravity to the tale he heard. He was not thinking of the ability or reputation of his junior partner, but of a friendship of earlier years with a man who had been long dead. These were his two sons, and one had come to a violent death, and the other, it seemed, would be almost certainly hanged—and the boy had not seemed to be of that sort at all. But—you never can tell! A lawyer learns that well enough, as he deals with the follies and crimes of men.

He said gently: "It can't make much difference, can it? You see, he was shot in the back. It would be hard to get over that."

"Yes, I daresay it would. You couldn't call it an easy case, at the best. But we might have cooked something up. It's wonderful what you can do, when you know just what you've got to explain away. And the remand gives us a week. At the worst, we could have fought for manslaughter, and for a reprieve after that. But—when he denies what they can prove up to the hilt! It gives us no chance at all."

"I shouldn't attach too much importance to that. I mean, to the statement which you have already made. It's not much more than a general denial. As you say, you've got a week. I've no doubt he'll talk differently when he's had time to think it over, and you've put it to him in the right light. Are you satisfied that you know what the case against him really is?"

"Yes, I think I do. There's the post-mortem report still to come, and a few details that aren't clear, but Inspector Byfleet has been very decent. He said they'd nothing they wished to keep back. I think he'd help us if we'd got any real defence to set up—I mean anything to extenuate or reduce the charge. But if we just deny everything—well, it doesn't need saying. It's too silly for words. I suppose we ought to decline to go on with the case unless he'll take our advice."

"I don't think we can quite do that. We've been the Truscotts' lawyers too long. And your father, as I needn't remind you, was joint trustee with Rowton until he died. If he'd lived, things might have turned out in a different way. I don't suppose their father thought sufficiently what the position would be if Rowton were left with a free hand. But I believe he trusted him more than may have been wise. We were all younger then."

"You don't mean that you think Rowton's had any hand in this?"

"No. It would be absurd. But I wish you'd tell me just how much Roger admits, and where his denials begin."

"You might say he admits everything up to the very time that the shot was fired, or perhaps three minutes before. He doesn't deny anything till they're both on the spot, with the witnesses all about, and then he says that he wasn't there! It's like refusing to plead."

"How can he say that he wasn't there?"

"He says he went out first, and left Cyril behind."

"And why shouldn't that be true?"

"Because they were seen to go out together. There are three witnesses to that, and there might as well be three dozen. There would have been, if it hadn't been just after one, and most of the staff gone to lunch. They saw Cyril go out in a rage—they all agree about that—cursing his brother as he went, and calling out that he wouldn't listen to any more. He went out at a door which opens on to a small stone landing, about two yards square, with the stairs in front of it. There's no other door—nothing. Just the stairs—and the street door at the foot. Roger followed him out, just a few yards behind, closing the door as he went. They heard loud voices but not words, and then the sound of a shot. They ran to find out what had happened, and one of them—a clerk named Menzies—was in time to see Roger disappear through the street door. He left his brother dead at the foot of the stairs. He'd got a bullet through the back, and a broken neck. He must have fallen most of the way down. And Roger simply says that he wasn't there."

"And this account of what happened earlier is not in dispute? Does it give any adequate motive for such a crime?"

"Not adequate. It gives some. And as to denying it, there isn't much that he could. Though in view of what he does deny, perhaps I shouldn't say that.

"But he couldn't deny that he'd been having a difference with his brother about letting the shares go, because we've been having that over with him here every day for the last week. And though we advised a sale on the facts that Mr. Rowton had given us, and the certified figures from Bagley's office, I don't say that he hadn't made me a bit doubtful whether there wasn't some dirty work going on in the rear. If he'd brought his brother here yesterday afternoon, as I'd asked him to do, I'd got a suggestion to make that might have settled the whole thing, one way or other, but it's too late for that now.

"Anyway, he'd written to Cyril to say that he wouldn't sell, and telling him that it was no use coming up to town again, as he wouldn't alter his mind. It wouldn't be any good to deny that, because the police have got the typist's notebook in which it was taken down. It's quite a reasonable letter. They let me see a copy at the police station.

"However, Cyril wouldn't take that. He came up on Tuesday night, and they had a talk at his hotel then. After that, Cyril went out by himself, and there's a suggestion, which may be true, that he got a bit wild. They say that he didn't seem more than half sober when he came to Cannon Street yesterday morning. That may go some way to explain what happened afterwards. He probably bullied and threatened, and Roger may have been frightened of him, and lost his head. It's no excuse, but it may go some way towards an explanation."

"It sounds weak to me—particularly in view of how the shooting is said to have happened," Mr. Weatherhead said doubtfully.

"So it is. Weak as a kitten. But a poor explanation may be better than none."

"Or it may be worse. It may prevent sufficient search for the true one."

"Yes, that's right enough. But the explanation's something we oughtn't to have to guess. We ought to get that from our client. He's the one man who knows. We can't help those who won't help themselves."

"What about the gun? I should have thought that Roger would be very unlikely to have one at all."

"So should I. I haven't had time to go into that yet. I don't suppose the police have either. But what use is it, while he denies the whole thing? It may be it was Cyril's gun, and he first pulled it on him, and Roger wrenched it away, and fired in a sudden impulse as Cyril turned to run down the stairs. Even panic might explain that. The finger contracts on the trigger, almost without intention. You can twist facts a dozen ways, but you can't do much with facts that you haven't got. We ought to know how he got that gun, and be ready to explain why, and why he'd got it with him yesterday.

"But it's no use making anything up, such as saying that it must have been Cyril's gun, when the police may put the man in the box from whom Roger bought it the night before."

"We don't want to make anything up," Mr. Weatherhead replied. "We want to be sure that the truth is put to the court in the best way. And we ought to assume that our client's instructions are true, until the contrary is decided."

"But we know some of it isn't."

"Perhaps so. You must see him again, when he's had time to adjust his mind. Had he got a licence to carry a gun?"

"No. Inspector Byfleet says there'll be a charge about that, but it will be left on the file till they've disposed of the present one. I suppose they're so sure of a conviction that they don't think it's worth while to proceed with anything else."

"Well, they may be right. You don't seem to have an easy case. But there's another reason why they must let the lesser charge stand over.

"They can't assume that he did carry the gun. It might be much harder to prove than the murder charge they have made. As you say, he might have snatched it from Cyril's hand."

"Well, we oughtn't to sit guessing here. He ought to tell us all this, and then I might get busy to give him some real help."

Mr. Weatherhead made no further reply. His attention seemed to have wandered. He sat gazing into the fire, his thoughts going back to the days which his young partner had never known. After a time, he said: "There's one thing you mustn't forget. It mayn't seem very important now, but it's a matter we oughtn't to overlook. I mean the question of selling the shares. The present offer expires tomorrow."

"You think the shares ought to be sold?"

"Yes, I think there's no option now. It seemed wise to us at the first, and Boddington took the same view. And suppose Roger Truscott were right in thinking that there was some misrepresentation or trickery—it isn't very clear what, and I don't think he was overcompetent to decide—I should still give the same advice. If he escaped with a long-term sentence, which seems the best we can hope, his interests would be absolutely in Rowton's hands.

"Even if you say Rowton's a rogue—and we've got no proof that goes anything like so far—I should still give the same advice.

It's £30,000 to be had clear of risk, and we should be best out of his hands.

"And it's—yes, it's all Roger's, now Cyril's dead. But there couldn't be sufficient motive in that?"

"You'd think not. But it's curious how often, when someone gets poisoned or shot, there's someone about three feet away who picks up what he drops. It seems to act like a natural law."

"Yes," the older man said more tolerantly, "we've all noticed that at times. But it mayn't be quite what it sounds. A man's closest relatives are likely to be round him when he is sick, and they are the ones who most often benefit by his death."

Leslie did not dispute that. He said: "Anyway, you've given me an idea. I'll arrange to see Roger at once, and take his instructions to sell the shares. He can't be fool enough to stand out about that now. He'll want money for his defence. Perhaps I'd better rub it in, if he tries playing the mule any more."

"I shouldn't anticipate that, if I were you. We've got to do all we can, for his father's sake, if not for his own."

Leslie added mentally: "and for the sake of the firm too." He could not feel much concern for a dead man he had never known, and any pity he might have had for his son was deadened by the exasperation he felt at the stubborn folly which would not admit that which it was so plainly vain to deny.

Mr. Weatherhead rose rather stiffly from the fireside seat, and went back to his desk. He would do no good to anyone by neglecting his own work. And he did not think it likely that Roger would remain obstinate in that useless denial. He had seen too often the difference which results from a few hours in a quiet cell.

CHAPTER IX.

INSPECTOR BYFLEET made no difficulty about arranging for Mr. Tonks to visit his client that afternoon. It is the routine of such cases to give reasonable facilities for defending lawyers to consult their clients, and in this instance, the Inspector could afford to be generous. He had rarely had a simpler case, nor one in which a conviction would be more certain. Besides, he was one of those officers of the law, perhaps more numerous in fact than in popular imagination, who are more concerned that an indictment should be equitably presented to the court than with the result which may follow, and in this case he had formed the opinion that there was something—possibly, something of importance to the accused—that he did not know.

"It's a cold-blooded, brutal murder, Mr. Tonks," he said bluntly. "I don't see how you'll get over that; and I don't suppose you'll make much of a try. But I'm not satisfied all the same. There's motive, but not motive enough. It's not natural somehow. I mean, I can't help feeling that there's something we're not on the track of yet, and, of course, that's where you come in. I've got the postmortem report. You can have a copy of that. But I don't see that it's going to be any good to you. Bullet entered at the back, a little to the left of the spine, penetrated lung and left ventricle of the heart, in a slightly downward direction, probably fired by someone standing above, though not much, and holding the gun not less than three feet away. Suicide is therefore impossible—bleeding mostly internal. Broken neck and other injuries, the severity of which indicates that he fell the whole length of the stairs. Either of the major injuries would have caused almost instant death, and it is therefore difficult to give either the preference. There's the whole thing put in simpler words than any doctor would care to use.

"Your client shot his own brother in the back, and went out to eat a good lunch. He'd just finished when I asked him to step this way, and I stood by while he paid the bill. There's no getting over

46

that. But it makes me think that there's something more that we don't know. Unless of course, he's insane, which I'm told he's not."

"He would be, if he'd killed his brother the way you say," Leslie announced boldly, "but you know what our defence is. We say we didn't fire the shot, and don't know who did, because we left first."

There was a slight twinkle in the Inspector's eyes as he answered: "Well, it's his funeral, not ours. But you'll have to get up early to make a jury believe that."

"I don't care how early I get up, but that's what we say, and that's what we mean to prove," the lawyer answered, with a tone of confidence which he did not feel. It actually caused Inspector Byfleet to turn his experienced mind, when he had left, to a careful scrutiny of the evidence in his possession for any possible weakness; but he found it complete and final, "unless," as he said to himself, with a quiet smile, "there should be a secret door on the stairs. Perhaps we ought to tap the walls to dispose of that possibility! But, all the same, there's something here that we don't know."

Mr. Tonks met his client in the room reserved for such interviews. Roger was pale but self-controlled, and obviously glad to see him. There had, indeed, been a pleasant acquaintance between the two men, approaching intimacy at times during the past week, for Roger had called several times at the lawyer's office to obtain advice on the legal problems that he confronted, and to discuss his doubts concerning the offer which he was being urged to accept, and conversation had wandered to the discovery of several congenial topics of common interest.

"I'm glad," he said, "that you've been able to come so soon. It seems to me that I'm in a very difficult position unless we can find out who shot Cyril, and, in any case, I shouldn't rest till I had."

"Yes, I'm afraid you are," was the rather dry reply. "Inspector Byfleet says he has three witnesses who saw you go out just behind your brother, and heard the shot."

"I think that must be a lie."

"I don't think so. Most of the staff had gone to lunch, but these three were still there. One of them got to the top of the stairs in time to see you leave by the street door. Menzies, his name was."

"He says I left after Cyril was shot? That's a lie, anyway."

"It isn't likely that everyone's telling lies. Why not say that he saw someone else, and thought it was you?"

"That's possible, of course."

"I don't know that it is. But it has a more plausible sound. The real difficulty is in the time. They were not far from the door, and

47

they ran to it at once when they heard the shot. Whoever fired it must have been at the top of the stairs when he pulled the trigger. You can work it out for yourself."

Roger looked at him in a moment of quiet silence. "You mean," he asked, "that you don't believe what I say?"

"I haven't said that. There are other possibilities. At least, you may not intend to mislead me. There are instances of loss of memory following shock."

"I hadn't had any shock. That's come since. Do you really think that I should have shot Cyril dead, and then walked out to lunch as though nothing had happened? Why, I never even handled a gun in my life, let alone having one."

"The question isn't what I think. The trouble is that several witnesses saw you, and that's what they say you did. As to the lunch, Inspector Byfleet himself is a witness to that."

"Have you ever thought how a sane man must feel when he's shut up in an asylum, and knows his business is being ruined, and perhaps his wife going off with another man, and he knows that if he shows any excitement it will be taken as evidence that his lunacy's rather more dangerous than usual? Well, that's how I feel now. I can see I'm in a more difficult position than I realised even half-an-hour ago. I've got no chance unless I keep calm, and it isn't easy to do. Are you willing to handle this case for me on the assumption that I am right when I say that I went out before Cyril and not after?"

"No. I don't know that I am."

"Then, I must find someone else who is."

"Mr. Weatherhead was anxious that I shouldn't throw up the case. He thought you might look at matters differently when you'd had more time for consideration. I'm bound to advise you that I think it's a useless line of defence. It's worse than that, because it shuts our mouths from offering any explanation that might put the case in a better light than the prosecution will be likely to do."

"You mean you think that I shot Cyril?"

"It doesn't really matter what I think. What matters is that there are three witnesses to swear that you did."

"It matters everything what you think. If you think you know the truth now, you won't try to find it out, and what can I do, shut up here? It's an infamous thing that a man accused in this way should be shut up so that he can't do anything for his own defence. But I made up my mind to keep calm."

"Well, suppose we leave that for a moment. There's another matter of even greater urgency. We've got a week before the case comes up again, but there's this share matter, and the offer expires on the 15th—that's tomorrow—and Mr. Weatherhead thinks that, under the present circumstances, you'll do best to accept."

"I don't intend to do that."

"What can you do better, placed as you are?"

"How long do you suppose I'm going to stay here?"

"I wish I could answer that. You know we'll do all we can. But, meanwhile, you can get this money clear of all risks, and, if you don't, you're absolutely in Rowton's hands, whom you don't trust; and, if the business goes wrong, he'll always be able to say that he showed you a way out that you wouldn't take, and so you ruined yourself and everyone else as well."

"I can't help what anyone says, but I made up my mind that I shouldn't sell, and I'm not going to change because I've been got into this mess."

"I think you're the most obstinate man that I ever met. Do you realise that, if this case should go to trial, as it almost certainly will, you'll need funds for your own defence?"

"Perhaps I shall, but as you decline to defend me in any sensible way—"

"I haven't declined anything yet. Suppose I bring the deed here tomorrow—I shall have to come rather early, being Saturday, if any business is to be got through—and you can think things over again between now and then? We've both got rather warmed up. By the way, do you seriously say that it wasn't your gun?"

"I've told you that I never had or handled one in my life."

"Was it Cyril's?"

"How can I tell? I don't believe he ever had one either. I never heard of it, if he had."

"Then you think I couldn't possibly do you any harm if I press the police to use all their resources to trace the origin of the weapon?"

"Of course you can't. That's the first word of sense I've heard since you came in. But, if they know their business, surely they'd do that, whether you ask them or not."

"I daresay they would. But if they think they've got a clear case, they mightn't go very far, especially if they think it's your gun."

"Well, you must take it from me that it never was. Can't you see that I've got too much at stake to tell you what isn't true?"

Leslie Tonks went away in some doubt of mind. Was it possible that three witnesses could be wrong in so clear a tale? But Roger's final argument became less convincing as he pondered upon it. Criminals who had so much at stake did not always think that the truth would be useful to set them free.

CHAPTER X.

It was after Mr. Weatherhead's usual time for leaving when the junior partner got back to the offices of the firm, but he found him to be still there, having waited to hear his report of the afternoon's interview.

He listened to this without comment, only asking an occasional question to clarify the narrative in his own mind, until Leslie concluded with the remark: "Of course, I know it's absurd, but the fact is that when he protested that he hadn't shot Cyril, and didn't know who had, and hadn't even handled a gun in his life, I half began to wonder whether he wasn't speaking the truth. And Inspector Byfleet has much the same feeling. At least, he said he was inclined to think that there was something more to come out."

"But that isn't much the same as suggesting that Roger may not have done it," Mr. Weatherhead objected. "Inspector Byfleet is a very experienced officer. His opinion is not one to be lightly put aside. But I should say that what he meant was that while there can be no doubt that Cyril Truscott died by his brother's hand, yet there is some complication of motive or emotion to which we have no clue in the facts as they are yet known.

"I've been thinking it over this afternoon while you've been away—I've had a little experience myself in the last forty-five years—and I came to the same conclusion. But I came to another, which seems to be about opposite to your own. You think Roger shot his brother. So far we agree. You go on to think that it's a rather stupid obstinacy that makes him stick to his tale that he left before it occurred, because you think it's one that no jury would swallow.

"I don't say that you're wrong there, but has it occurred to you that a small chance is better than none?

"If he once admits that it was his hand that fired the shot, do you think there's any tale that ingenuity could invent that would be sufficient to save his neck? A brother—shot in the back—when he

50

was going away—shot with the only gun that there was. The best counsel that was ever briefed might come down at a fence like that.

"Isn't it his one chance—call it as small as you will—to stick out to the last that he went out first, and to rely on us to shake the testimony of the witnesses, to impugn their memories—if not their veracities—to raise a doubt in the jury's mind?

"I'm not sure that his instinct hasn't been right about that, and when you've been urging him to admit that it was the work of his own hand, that you haven't been urging him to pull the rope more tightly round his neck."

"Well," Leslie said frankly, "I hadn't thought of it in that way; but I'm not sure that you're wrong. What course ought I to steer now, if we take that view?"

"I think there's no doubt about that. You've urged him already to admit that he fired the shot, and to try to explain it away, and he's refused to take your advice. If he goes his own way now, and he finds himself in the ditch, he can blame himself, but not you.

"But if you find he stands out tomorrow to the same tale, I think you ought to accept it, as long as you don't know that it isn't true, which you certainly don't as yet. You ought to let him see that you mean to work on those lines, and search every scrap of contrary evidence for whatever flaws you can find. It's a fighting chance, though it's small—and it seems to me it's the only one that there is."

Having delivered himself of this opinion, Mr. Weatherhead rose to make his way to his waiting car. As he put on his coat, he added: "And, by the way, if you find he's still obstinate about selling the shares, you can tell him that he needn't worry about funds. I'll see him through that, for his father's sake, if not for his own."

"You mean you don't think he ought to sell out?"

"No. I think he should. If he's made up his mind that way, you can just say nothing, and let him sign. But I don't want him to sell against his own wish because he thinks he can't get defended unless he does."

"As you say, of course. But it's a fairly big risk. Counsel's fees in a case like this—"

"I dare say we shall find that much in Truscott's at the worst, if we start to dig. But it's my risk, not the firm's."

CHAPTER XI.

THE next morning, having had the benefit of a night's reflection, during which he had adjusted his mind to recognise the force of the advice which he had received from his more experienced partner, Leslie Tonks had a second and more satisfactory interview with a difficult client.

He commenced, in accordance with his partner's wishes, by producing, as though for signature, the deed which would have surrendered possession of Roger Truscott's heritage in his father's business. He had requested its return from Bagley & Co.'s office on the previous day, and had doubtless led Mr. Boddington to conclude that he was obtaining its execution, as the only one who could readily achieve access to Roger, under existing circumstances; and as a means (Mr. Boddington would suppose) by which funds could be found for the hopeless, spectacular battle of the defence.

Roger, looking weary from the long misery of a sleepless night, greeted him quietly, and said, as he drew out the document: "I suppose you want me to sign that? Well, so I will, if we can agree on the lines on which we are going ahead rather better than we did yesterday."

"I hope that you see now that it's the wisest course."

"No. I don't at all. I do it under protest, on your advice, and because I'm more or less in your hands. I don't believe that the business would go down if we carried on, and I believe the shares would soon be worth four times what we're offered now. But you'll say," he added, the momentary energy dying out of his voice, "that I've other things to think about now, and the business has got to go."

"You've got other things to think about. I can't deny that. But if you don't want to sell the shares, Mr. Weatherhead asked me to say that there'll be no difficulty about funds. The firm will advance any sum that's required, and you can have any counsel who's free to accept the brief."

"I don't want counsel who won't believe what I say."

"Counsel usually do that, or at least they take the line of defence set up in the brief, if they accept it at all. I don't say that some might not return it, if they should find they'd have to take up grounds that they disapprove."

"The only line of defence is that I didn't do it, or even know it was done, and that there's no one alive who's more eager to learn the truth."

"Very well. We are prepared to accept that. You realise the consequence must be that we shall start investigations, and cross-examine witnesses, on that assumption—that, for instance, we shall move heaven and earth, if necessary, and perhaps request the aid of the police, to trace the ownership of the revolver, and how it came to be there?

"And there's another consequence that we can't avoid. The prosecution, in endeavouring to fasten the murder upon you, may put it in the worst possible light, and we're shut out from reply. We can't suggest any extenuating provocation, any threat, any accident—in fact, instigation of any kind. They'll say that you must have deliberately brought the gun with you, and that you shot your own brother in the back when you were alone with him on the stairs, thinking that you could escape into the street before the discovery of the crime, so that no one could ever prove that the act was yours. And to that our only reply will be that you were not the one who fired the shot, and that all the witnesses must be making mistakes—unless you want us to say that they have combined to lie."

Roger Truscott listened to this warning with a pale face, and, as he was not quick to reply, Leslie thought for a moment that he was about to hear some dramatic confession, with such explanation (truthful or otherwise) as the ingenuity of a cornered criminal could contrive to offer.

But when he spoke he said quietly: "Yes, I see all that. But what else can I do? I want you to find out the truth by every means in your power."

"Very well. That's agreed. You can reckon from now on that we put every other thought from our minds. You didn't shoot Cyril. You went out first. You never owned nor even saw the gun with which he was shot. We stand or fall on that, and we don't mean to fall if there's any human way by which we can pull you through. We've got a week, and now we've agreed what the plan of campaign must be, there won't be a day lost: you can be quite sure about that.

"But, just to get it out of the way, what do you mean to do about this agreement? I don't want to influence you one way or other. But it's got to be signed, and sent over this morning, if it's to be any use doing it."

"If you don't press me, I shan't sign."

"Then that's that. And the next question is, do you want counsel briefed for when the case comes on again, and, if so, have you any choice of who you're to have?"

"I've no idea about that. I should leave it to you to decide. I suppose it needn't be settled today?"

"No, if you leave it to us. Now I want you to tell me just what happened on Wednesday. Or from the night before, when Cyril came up, which he seems to have done as soon as he got your letter—by the way, the police have a copy of that, from the typist's book."

"Well, that doesn't matter. It only told him there'd be no sense in his coming up on Wednesday, as there'd be nothing to pick up. I said I'd decided not to sell, and he must take that as final; and I gave him a few reasons why. But I didn't waste many words over them, because I didn't expect him to agree, nor to care much whether they were bad or good. He only wanted the cash. Oh, and I said I could arrange to find him some money at once, if he needed it. I'd asked the bank about that."

"Yes, I've seen the letter—that is, a copy. I think you've remembered it accurately enough. It was quite a reasonable letter to write, and it gets us just this far forward—which isn't much—that you couldn't have formed any plan of murdering him then, as you didn't encourage him to come up to town. Did you expect he would, after he'd read it?"

"Yes, I thought it more likely than not. I hoped he wouldn't, but I expected he would. I knew he'd think me a fool, and be angry at the delay in getting his money, even if he didn't honestly think that I was doing the wrong thing; but I didn't guess how savage he'd be."

"You never got on very well with him?"

"No. We used to be friendly at times, and we quarrelled, as brothers do—and forgot it and were friendly again. But we hadn't many interests in common. I never cared for sports, and I suppose we both despised the other more than we should for being so different, but we were friends underneath. You see, we had no near relatives living. We might quarrel between ourselves, but we should have been side by side against any attack against either. That is how I should have put it a week ago. I'll own Cyril lost his head over this money. It's a large sum, and he honestly thought me an utter fool, as perhaps I am. And I've no doubt it must be exasperating to have a brother eighteen months older who can settle your affairs for you, and perhaps ruin you, whether you like it or not. I don't say he didn't lose his head, and say a lot more than he meant, which may have been overheard; but no one can say that I ever made a threat against him. I hadn't any such thought. I'd no cause, and it isn't sense. But what I meant to say was this, that however he felt, if anyone had murdered me, he'd have been on his track till he ran him down, and I feel the same about him, or, at least, I should have done if I hadn't been caught in this nightmare way—and if you ask me to explain it, it's something I can't do, any more than you can yourself. Indeed, I expect you know more about it than I—I don't even know who the people are who are supposed to have seen what happened, or what the case is that we've got to meet."

Leslie listened to this without interruption. He wanted Roger to talk, and was content to bring him back to the point when he had wandered from it as far as his inclination led. And, as he listened, a real doubt came to his mind. The idea that Roger might be innocent took a reality which was quite different from the professional belief which he had previously undertaken to feel. And with this genuine doubt, there came a faint, inadequate realisation of what it must be to be caught thus in the trap of circumstance, so that life and honour may go down to a common pit.

"We can't know that with any finality till the prosecution have presented their case, and we hear what their witnesses say, and see how they stand up to cross-examination. But if you didn't shoot Cyril, someone else did, and it's our business to find out who. We're not bound to, of course. We're not bound, even, to show you're innocent. It's their business to prove their case. That's the theory of the legal position. But it doesn't work out like that, particularly in murder trials. I don't suppose it ever did, and it certainly doesn't since the accused is expected to go into the witness box, and counsel is allowed to comment on it, if he doesn't. But there must be someone who fired that shot, and we've got a week in which to give him a name. You might go on telling me what happened when Cyril came."

"He came on Tuesday. He must have wired me as soon as he got my letter in the morning."

"Wired you? What did he say? I suppose the police have got that?"

"No. I tore it up."

"Well, the original could be got from the post office. But I don't see why the police should get on the track of it. The question mightn't arise. But what we've got to consider is whether it would do us any good. What did it say?"

"It said, as nearly as I can remember, 'Strongest protest against your action shall hold you responsible to last penny if I lose through your obstinacy coming immediately do nothing till I arrive.' He rang me up at the office about three o'clock, and I arranged to meet him at his hotel at four."

"Just a moment. I want to get that wire down. Your brother didn't spare words."

"No. He never counted what he spent. That was half the trouble. He could get any credit he needed, because we were supposed to be heirs to a wealthy business, and very rich. I used to suppose that myself up to ten days ago, and never really troubled about his debts. But he was in debt rather heavily, although he'd always borrowed about half my allowance, and he must have owed me nearly £600 when he died."

"And you were willing to let him have more?"

"I offered him £500 when I met him at the hotel. I told him that I asked the bank, and they'd go that far against a deposit of shares, but no more. They said it wasn't the kind of advance that their Board approved, especially as the money was not required for any commercial purpose, and for a somewhat prolonged or indefinite period. I told him that, if he saw me at the office next morning, he could have the money."

"Did he have it?"

"No. He said he wasn't going to make any such deal. He knew where he could get £500, if he wanted it, without any favours from me."

"Then it wasn't to get money from you that he saw you again next day?"

"No. Not except by the sale of the shares, to which he was still trying to persuade me to agree."

"Could he have got money elsewhere, or was it no more than a boast?"

"He had a friend, a son of Dowson, the brewer, from whom he got money rather easily. He may have been thinking of him."

"So, in fact, he had no money from you, although you offered it? It isn't a case of him having a large sum on him, and having been shot and robbed?"

"No. I don't think robbery seems a probable motive, it happening how and when it did. But then nothing about it does seem probable. Though it isn't quite correct that he had no money from me. I didn't mean to say that. I took £20 with me on Tuesday afternoon, which was all I could spare till the month's end, and he had that, though he wouldn't agree to the larger sum."

"Then the question of whether he was robbed may be worth considering. I saw a list of the contents of his pockets. There was a return ticket to Oxford, and quite a small amount of cash. I think it was £2 4s. 0d. Did you give him the money in banknotes, or how?"

"It was in one-pound notes. But I don't think he was robbed. He wouldn't be likely to have much of the money left after the sort of evening he'd probably had."

"You mean it would have been of an expensive, and probably discreditable, kind?"

"It would be—hilarious. He reckoned on having what he called a lively time when he came up to town. It was quite common for him to run through a good deal of money on such occasions."

"Do you know how it went? Women, gambling, or what?"

"Not at all definitely. There were some matters on which we were not at all confidential. I suppose he thought I should disapprove."

"What I'm trying to get at is whether he could have formed some acquaintances, or got into some row the night before, which resulted in this crime the next day."

"Yes. I see. But I can't help you there. I wish I could."

"Suppose he had incurred a debt—gambling, for instance—and arranged for someone to meet him at your office to pay it off. We must follow that up, though it isn't easy to see how it fits some of the facts, if we can call anything a fact yet. But what I'm most anxious to know is what happened at the offices, when he saw you there, and when you both left."

"There's not much to tell, beyond what I suppose you'll have heard before now.

"He wasn't quite himself—I don't mean that he was less than sober, but he was in a state of bad temper and irritation that wasn't unusual when he'd had a late night, and I suppose he'd had one or two more drinks in the effort to pull himself together again. He was furious with me because I wouldn't give way, and he talked in a manner that I don't suppose he would if he'd been more like his normal self, and some things he said must have been overheard."

"Could any threat have been overheard—any angry retort—anything that could be taken hold of—that you made in reply?"

"No. I didn't make any. I'm certain of that. If anyone says that, it's untrue."

"I don't know that they have. As your brother was in the mood you describe, could he have quarrelled with anyone else on the premises? Did he talk to anyone beside you?"

"He talked to Mr. Rowton. He was in his office for some time, and the three of us were together for a few minutes, but there was no quarrelling about that. Rowton was explaining to him that he'd done all he could to persuade me to a different decision, but he'd given it up in despair. They were in agreement against me."

"Did Rowton make a fresh effort to talk you over, when he found he'd got your brother's support?"

"Not much. He took the line that he'd done all he could, and that there was nothing left but to give in to my point of view, and do our best to pull together to carry the business on. He spoke as though he'd given up, but he'd be very glad if Cyril could be more persuasive."

"And how did you part at last? You need to be very careful here, for this is the vital point."

"I said I'd got to go out to lunch, and it wasn't any use going on talking. We'd got to the point where we were saying the same thing over and over again. It must have been before one when I said that, because it was after that that the office began to clear. But he wouldn't go. He said he didn't mean to stop till he'd got my word that he would have his money—that was how he talked of it, as though I'd already got £15,000 of his that I wouldn't hand over, and I said at last, if he wouldn't go, would he come out and have lunch together?

"Then he turned round, and said if I were with him it would make him too sick to eat. He'd come out, if he had my word first that he'd have his money. So then I said if he wasn't going, I was, and I came away."

"There was no quarrel beyond that at the last moment? No altercation that might have been misconstrued in the light of what happened afterwards?"

"I pushed past him. Nothing beyond that. He could have stopped me, if he had really meant to. He's stronger than I. The last words between us may have been overheard. He followed me out of my room into the—well, it's rather hard to describe, it's like an extension of the general office, but out of sight of the clerks that are working there, that I had to cross to get to the door at the head of the private stairs—and Mr. Rowton was coming out of his room at the same time.

"I think Cyril's last words were that I could go where I liked, but I'd find him there when I got back. Rowton may have heard that. I came away without looking round. I didn't see anyone else there. I believe Cyril and Mr. Rowton were talking as I left, but I couldn't honestly swear to that. I went to lunch at my usual place, and I'd just finished when Inspector Byfleet arrested me for murdering Cyril."

"You didn't even know that Cyril followed you down?"

"No. And I doubt whether he did."

"The trouble is that the police appear to think there's conclusive evidence about that. Can you say how many minutes after one it was when you left? That may become a vital point, because it can't have been long after one that the murder occurred."

"I should say it was about five minutes past. I should have said it might be a minute earlier, or perhaps two, but I remember seeing that the restaurant clock was at ten past when I sat down, and I think I should get there within five minutes."

"But you don't know that it was correct to a minute, which is less likely than not. For the moment, we will assume that you left at four minutes past. It will be important to ascertain just how much interval there was between then and the moment when the police were summoned, which is understood to have been instantly after the crime was committed."

As he said that, Leslie rose to go. He shook hands with a cordiality which he would not have shown on the previous day. The case had taken hold of him now, so that he believed the tale he had heard, and felt that he was allied with his client in refuting a monstrous charge, though he was still in the dark, not only as to how he could uncover the truth, but as to what its revelation would be likely to show.

He noticed that Roger had an increased cheerfulness, a more confident aspect, now that his protest of ignorance had been adopted as the basis on which the defence was to be prepared; and he was shrewd enough to reflect that this increased the probability that it was a genuine presentation. He picked up the unsigned deed, which was lying on the bare deal table between them.

"I must let Boddington know," he said, "that we shall not execute this," and so turned, without further wasting of words, to summon the constable who was waiting outside the door of the cell. He heard the key shot, as he walked away.

It is the constant experience of a criminal lawyer to be a part of tragedies which he does not share, but, he reflected—who would have thought it a week ago?

CHAPTER XII.

It was a few minutes to one when Leslie got back to his own offices, which, it being Saturday morning, were already vacated except for the telephone operator, and a junior clerk who was waiting to dispatch some letters which were on his desk for signature.

As he sat down to deal with them, the telephone rang, and he picked it up to learn that Mr. Boddington was on the wire.

"Put him through," he said, and heard the accountant's voice: "About Truscott & Rowton—I promised to let Mr. Rowton know whether your client had signed. I didn't suppose there was any doubt, but I thought I'd better ring you up, so that I could write him definitely."

"No, he hasn't. He says he told Rowton that he had made up his mind about that."

There was a moment's silence, and then: "Well, it's a suicidal folly. I suppose you've no more influence over him than anyone else; but I should have thought under existing circumstances—"

"But I have no wish to influence him," Leslie replied, with a decision of tone which was almost curt, "it is a course of which I fully approve."

He laid down the receiver. It was not an opinion which he would have expressed yesterday. Even earlier in the week, when his talks with Roger had somewhat shaken his previous confidence in the wisdom of the proposed sale, and before the position had been complicated and jeopardised by an accusation of murder against his client which it might not be easy to rebut, he would not have committed himself to so assured a statement. The change showed that, perhaps beyond his own consciousness, he was identifying himself with his client's cause and his client's mind.

But there was nothing more to be done now. Nothing till Monday, except to consider the facts he had, and to make his plans.

He must trace the ownership of the revolver, which, as it was in the possession of the police, could not be done without their cooperation. He no longer feared that he might be manufacturing evidence against his client by urging such an enquiry. But he felt a decided reluctance to saying anything to Inspector Byfleet which would indicate the line of defence which he intended to take. If the police thought that they had a walkover with the evidence they already had, and that the defence would be no better than some fantastic tale of impossible accident, or of a weapon that went off in a struggle and shot its owner—(in the back!)—well, let them remain in that soporific delusion. If the tale that they had was false, it could not be of an unshakable strength, and a false tale is most vulnerable to an unexpected attack. He must try to collect material for its destruction without the prosecution having knowledge of what he did. And probably they were enquiring about the gun already. There is, as he knew, considerable thoroughness about the methods of the metropolitan police. Anyway, he could ask Byfleet whether they had settled the ownership of the gun, and see what he replied. He could do that without giving himself away. Possibly, he might leave it at that until after the next hearing.

And there were the three witnesses on whom the police relied. Rowton, Menzies, and a third whose name he did not yet know. They must be approached with caution, if at all. But with Rowton, at least, it would be natural to discuss the tragedy. And he could make other excuses to see him.

These thoughts passed through his mind as he was lunching before leaving the city, as he had decided that it would be too late to go home for that meal, according to his usual Saturday custom. Having considered it, he went back to his office, and typed with his own hand:

Dear Mr. Rowton,

Mr. Roger Truscott refused finally this morning to consent to a sale of the shares in your firm which he controls, and we must conclude that the offer to purchase has now lapsed.

We do not know whether you would be able to negotiate a short extension of time, but, in any event, we should be glad to discuss with you the position which will result from the withdrawal of the offer.

Could you give us a call on Monday morning, preferably between eleven and twelve?—and oblige.

Yours faithfully,

Tonks & Weatherhead, L.T.

He went home, having despatched this letter, feeling that he had made the first move toward the solution of the problem which was before him.

The letter duly reached Mr. Rowton's desk on Monday morning, and that gentleman read its concluding paragraphs with a satisfaction that mitigated the information it first contained.

He had no difficulty in resolving to give Mr. Tonks the interview he desired, but he very naturally decided that a conference with the firm's auditors would be an appropriate preliminary, and he called first upon Mr. Boddington, with whom he had a long talk which Miss Morton was not privileged to hear, as her employer found an excuse to occupy her in another part of the offices, which he would rarely do for any consideration of business reticence, having well-founded beliefs both in her loyalty and discretion, as has been already observed.

Arriving at the solicitor's offices slightly before the suggested time, Mr. Rowton found himself shown into Mr. Tonks' room very readily, and received by that gentleman with his usual affability.

"I'm sorry to have troubled you to call, on what I know must be a busy morning for you," he began, "but I thought that the fact that the offer to purchase the business, on which I know you have been relying for some months past, should have lapsed on Saturday; and the circumstances of last week, as affecting your two principal shareholders, rendered it desirable that I should have your views on the position as promptly as possible, so that I may be prepared to deal in the right way with any question that may arise."

"Yes," Mr. Rowton agreed, answering the earlier portion of the solicitor's explanation, "I must confess that I had not anticipated the present position. I had supposed for some time past that I should have to do no more than to keep the flag flying until Roger Truscott should come of age. I own that I didn't foresee the almost incredible obstinacy which has landed us where we are now. If he had been a businessman, I could have convinced him without difficulty that we'd got an offer that wasn't likely to come again—but what could be done with an inexperienced boy, who met everything he couldn't understand with the suspicion of ignorance?

"He wouldn't listen to you, nor to Boddington, and of course he wouldn't listen to me, and when his own brother came on the scene—"

He stopped, as though the remainder of the sentence was best unsaid, but the solicitor had a bolder appetite for explicit words.

"You think there's no doubt that Roger killed his brother?"

Mr. Rowton's reply paused. Then he answered slowly: "I don't want to say that. No one saw what occurred. But I suppose I ought to be frank with you, and if I am I'm bound to say that I can't see any other possible explanation. Of course, only Menzies saw him going out afterwards."

"Shall we say Menzies saw someone go out, and may have been mistaken as to who it was? It could only have been a moment's glimpse at the foot of the stairs."

"Yes. I told Menzies that, but he won't budge. He says he was sure. And, really, Mr. Tonks, if I'm frank with you, it doesn't rest upon that. The shot, which we all heard, came almost as soon as they'd gone through the door."

"Roger says that he went out first, and left without even knowing that his brother had been shot."

Mr. Rowton became silent again. There was reluctance in his voice when he replied: "Well, as to that, I'm sorry, but I can only say that it isn't my memory. Of course, there was provocation. I thought Roger was wrong to stand out as he did—you know that—but I'm not saying that that justified the way that Cyril behaved. I think you ought to go all out for manslaughter, and, if you fail in that, you ought to get a reprieve."

The solicitor gave no sign of dissenting from this advice. He went on: "Inspector Byfleet tells me that he has another witness, besides Menzies. I suppose there'd have been about fifty if it had happened ten minutes earlier?"

"Yes. At least there must have been a lot who would have heard the report. They wouldn't have actually seen them go out—not if they had been attending to their own work. But, when it happened, everyone had left, except Menzies, who had just come to my door to hand me a report that I'd told him to finish before he went off to lunch, and the porter, Bellman, who was beginning to clear up, as he always does at midday."

"Well, it's a bad business. But what we've got to discuss now is whether this plan of amalgamation is still open, or is the door finally shut—and, if it is, I want to know whether you think the business can be continued successfully on its own legs, or how serious the position is. Of course, I understand that there's no question of an immediate crisis. I want you to take a broad view. I'm asking you as the firm's solicitor, and also as representing the Truscott interest, which, as I needn't tell you, is four-fifths of the whole."

"I suppose you would be asking me that. In fact, I've had a talk with Boddington about the whole position this morning. When I had your letter, I thought it best to see him first, so that I could give you his views, as well as my own.

"I don't say we can't get an extension of a few days. We've got an unusually good reason for asking, in view of what happened last week, and Lessing's been very decent all along. Beside that, I think they'd rather pay something substantial to get control than go on competing with us to squeeze us out.

"But I think I ought to be frank with you regarding my own position. You know I've urged the acceptance of this offer from first to last, and I've done all I could to persuade Roger Truscott to the same view. I'll own that about the last thing I expected was that there would be such obstinacy from him.

"But it doesn't follow that it's been to my own advantage that the sale should go through. I don't say I shouldn't have done well enough. I should have had a ten-year appointment and a seat on the new board. You know all about that. But it doesn't follow that I cannot do better.

"You know the position in which I was left at Mr. Truscott's death. I was not only manager of the business, I was joint trustee with your father for the two sons. And when your father unexpectedly died, I was left sole trustee.

"Well, I think you'll say that I've done my part; but it's over now. After Roger Truscott comes of age, as he did this month, I'm free to give six months' notice to leave the firm, or, for that matter, I can be kicked out with the same notice."

"Yes, I know that. But it's not a thing that anyone is proposing to do."

"No. I reckon not. But it doesn't follow that, as things are, I mightn't feel free to go. You see, I'm Truscott & Rowton. Everyone knows I've controlled the business—you might say I've been the business—for seventeen years.

"I'll tell you this. If things hadn't gone as they have, and if Roger Truscott hadn't signed that deed, I meant to hand him my resignation this morning. In six months from now, he'd have had the pleasure of finding out what he could do with the business, with me on the other side. I'd done my best to save him, but, if he wouldn't listen, I didn't see why I should be drowned in the same boat.

"Now we're in the same position, except that there's no question of either of the young Truscotts' carrying on the business, even if they were capable. One's dead, and the other's likely to be in jail for a long time, if he gets nothing worse. I don't want to anticipate anything, and I know every man's innocent till the jury bring in the verdict, but, as businessmen, we are bound to look the facts in the face.

"I'll tell you what I'll do. It's what I've promised Boddington already, before I came here. I'll approach Lessing at once, and ask him to extend the offer till Wednesday next. I'll tell him that, as things happened, we haven't been able to get Roger Truscott's signature to the deed, and I'll make it a personal favour, if necessary, to get the extension.

"If I put it in that way, I've two or three reasons for thinking he won't refuse. But, if I do that, it's got to be quite definite. It must be a final yes or no on that day, or before. It's Roger Truscott's last chance, and, if he refuses it, you can't say that I haven't done all I could to save him from his own folly."

Mr. Tonks did not express any opinion on that point. He merely asked: "Then you'll ring me up as soon as you get Lessing's reply?"

Mr. Rowton departed, well content. He had no doubt that Tonks & Weatherhead would advise their client to sign now, and that they would have sufficient influence to enforce their opinion upon him. The costs of defending a capital charge are always high. They are apt to be scaled by nothing less than the possessions of the accused, whether little or much. And the shares were almost the whole of the Truscott estate. Mr. Leslie Tonks would be departing very widely from the caution which is the traditional characteristic of his profession, if he should let that £30,000 be jeopardised further in such a position, and after the friendly warnings that he had received.

Yet Mr. Tonks, thinking over the conversation in the quietude of his own office, found that that was what he was deciding to do.

CHAPTER XIII.

LESLIE TONKS sat for a few minutes after Mr. Rowton had left him, silently considering the information he had received. He soon dismissed the question of the sale of the business from a mind which must be occupied with even graver issues. He did not mean to do more than report the proposed extension of the offer to Roger Truscott (if it should be confirmed) and leave him to refuse it, as he felt sure that he would.

Meanwhile, let Rowton think what he pleased. On his own statement, he was not incurring any personal risk. Rather, he implied that he would be making a gesture of generosity if he concurred in the sale on the lines of the agreements already drafted. Well, perhaps it was a sacrifice which he would not be required to make.

It was more serious that he had made statements regarding Cyril Truscott's murder which it seemed impossible to reconcile with Roger's account, or even with his innocence of the crime. Believing in that innocence, as he was now honestly disposed to do, he must look on such a testimony with a very critical suspicion, directed both to the evidence itself and the quarter from which it came. It was true that it was said to be confirmed by two more or less independent witnesses, but he knew how often such statements will break down when they are challenged in the witness box, and he was not going to take them too seriously in view of his present belief that they could not be exactly true.

Yet he was disposed to the conclusion that it would be best that he should say and do nothing which would cast suspicion upon them until the moment should come when he could do so upon the records of the court. He saw that, if there were anything less than absolute honesty and candour in the offered testimony, to give warning of his doubt would be to give opportunity for rehearsal and examination, which might weld it into a more formidable substance.

Yet he saw that, at the least, the evidence might be more than could be successfully met by a mere denial, an unsupported statement that Roger had left before his brother, and had had no part in the tragedy. What was imperatively needed was to discover the truth of what had occurred in those fatal moments. Even a theory, however improbable, would be better than nothing, and, at present, even that was beyond his imagination.

But there were some things that could be done. He resolved to make excuse for another talk with Inspector Byfleet, and to set in hand some enquiries which could be better done by others than by himself.

By these means he obtained two pieces of information during the following day, the first of which was of a negative, and the second of a more positive character.

He learnt from Inspector Byfleet that the question of the ownership of the weapon which had been left at the side of the dying man, and was doubtless that with which the crime had been committed, had already engaged the attention of the police, but without anything being elicited by which either of the Truscott brothers could be connected with its possession. The Inspector said frankly that the information he had obtained was that neither of them was supposed to have any familiarity with firearms, or known to have had any in his possession at any time.

"But," he added, "I wouldn't say that's a point in his favour, for it makes it look as though he must have gone to some trouble to get the gun. A man who has always got one handy may let it off because he loses his temper, or thinks he's being attacked, and be sorry next minute for what he's done, but it's a different matter if he went out to buy it the night before. Not that I say anyone did, for that's rather more than we know yet, though I expect we soon shall."

"Then you haven't traced the ownership of the weapon?"

"No. And I don't say it's easy to do, unless we find that it was bought from a shop in the neighbourhood, which is the most probable thing."

"You mean it's not got any marks of identification? May I see it?"

"Yes. You've got a right to that."

He produced it from a drawer of his desk, and handed it across the table.

Leslie's acquaintance with such weapons was not extensive. He turned it over, and asked: "It's a foreign make, isn't it?" He had a passing thought that the explanation might be in that fact—that the murder had been committed by a foreigner, they being naturally mysterious, and of a notorious criminality. A Chinese mark on the barrel, and there would really have been nothing left to explain!

"Yes," the Inspector answered, "it's a pattern used very largely in the German army during the war. It is almost certainly one of that endless quantity of trophies brought back by our men when the war ended, and hidden away when it was made illegal to possess such firearms without special permission. But that doesn't carry us far."

"Doesn't it make it more likely that the murderer is a man who had it hidden away, than one who bought it for the occasion? Would this be the kind of weapon anyone asking for a revolver, and knowing little about them, would be sold at a London shop?"

"There's a small point there, though it's not much against the weight of evidence in the other scale."

"I think there may be more than a little. The Truscott boys were much too young to have been at the war, and, as far as my information goes, they had no relation from whom they could have received such a trophy."

Inspector Byfleet looked keenly at the lawyer. He did not attach any weight to the argument itself, but he saw implications.

"You're not really," he asked, "going to take the line that Roger Truscott's an innocent man?"

Leslie saw that he had gone nearer to showing his own hand than he had intended to do. The stronger the Inspector thought his case to be, and the less reason he had to expect that Roger's guilt would be seriously denied till the moment of hearing came, the better it would be for a defence which might have to depend upon nothing better than shaking the witnesses for the prosecution when its opportunity for cross-examination should arrive.

"I shall advise him to plead not guilty," he answered, "if you mean that. You will agree that that is the practically invariable custom when a capital charge has to be met. Beyond that, I haven't gone into the details sufficiently to decide how the case for the prosecution can best be answered."

"Well," the Inspector answered, "I've told you what our case is. It's not yet quite as complete as I like to make them, but it's cast-iron on the vital points. There's no doubt how Cyril Truscott died, nor by whose hand. You won't need advice from me, but I should say the best card in your pack is the fact that no one saw what took place on the stairs. You might do a lot with that but for the shot having been fired from behind."

Leslie said "Yes," noncommittally. He added: "I suppose there's no hope that anyone did see what happened?"

"You want to know whether we've got a witness who saw the shot? Then I'll tell you at once that we haven't, though a jury may decide—I've no doubt they will—that what we have got adds up to the same total. But I'm not going to spring any surprise on you such as that. I should tell you, if I had an actual witness of the murder. We don't try to score off the defence in such ways. Not in this kind of case, anyway. I don't think anyone living except Roger Truscott knows what happened in that two minutes on the stairs. No one has come forward to say that, and nobody ever will. But we've got another witness since yesterday. He's a tobacconist. He has a shop just by the street door, and he saw Roger come out. We didn't need him. He's a bit of overweight in a full scale."

"Did he hear the shot?"

"No. He says he didn't. But there's nothing surprising in that, when you consider the traffic, and the fact that the street door had been closed."

"Does he remember the time? The evidence wouldn't amount to much without that."

"Yes. He has a reason for being accurate. He was leaving his shop for a train which he caught at 1:10 P.M. He puts it at 1:05."

"And the time when the police were called in was—?"

"About 1:15."

Roger had the information he sought, and it had come by less direct enquiries than he had expected to have to use. He changed the subject to ask: "What about finger-marks on the gun?"

He knew he might be about to hear an answer which would transfer Roger's denial from the category of the improbable to the incredible, and he knew also that there was no possibility that the gun would not have been examined for such evidences, and it was best to know whatever he had to meet.

"There was none whatever."

The Inspector made this statement without comment, and it was to draw out his opinion that Leslie remarked: "That's rather in my client's favour. On the tale as you have it, he had no time for wiping the gun. He must have dropped it, and run."

"I couldn't agree with you there. It rather suggests deliberation. The gun must have been wiped clear of all previous finger-marks, and then used with a gloved hand."

Leslie made no reply to this, he thought he had learned all he could, and that with greater economy of confidence on his own side than he had thought that he could contrive. He got up to go, as he said: "Thanks for giving me so much information. I shall be glad to know if you succeed in tracing the gun. I must do what I can, but it isn't easy to make bricks without straw."

He felt the last remark to be one appropriate to the reserve which he had resolved to maintain, and yet which he could make with sincerity, for the available straw which was yet in sight was certainly of very meagre amount. Yet he walked away well satisfied with the result of the interview. He thought it possible that the new tobacconist witness might be of less use to the prosecution than the defence, and the facts he had learned about the weapon might also have been worse than they were. But his two main difficulties were still as formidable as before—the evidence of the three witnesses who had been at the top of the stairs, and the question of by whose hand, if not by Roger's, the crime had been committed.

He went to lunch, turning these things over in a mind that found little profit in the process, and returned to his office to learn that one of the enquiry agents whom he had put to work on the previous afternoon was waiting to see him.

The man, whose name was Evans, and who had something of the solemn and even sanctimonious manners and appearance commonly (and libellously) associated with dissenting deacons, sat down stiffly, and gave his report with some formality of diction, and an open notebook before him, which he did not appear to read, but to consult as though containing the texts on which his discourse was based.

"The time when Mr. Roger Truscott entered the Brading Restaurant on Wednesday, the 12th inst., can be proved with exactness, it being precisely ten minutes after one P.M. This will be sworn to by Mr. James Higham, a director of Higham and Rowbotham, Manchester Warehousemen, and the head of the London branch of that well-known house. This gentleman has been in the regular habit, for several years past, of lunching at the Brading Restaurant. He telephones his requirements at an earlier hour, and is served at 1:10 P.M., punctually upon his entrance, so that his time may not be wasted.

"I am informed by the headwaiter that he is a gentleman of extreme punctuality.

"On the day in question, Mr. Roger Truscott sat down at his table. The two gentlemen took their seats practically at the same instant. Mr. Higham is quite certain of that. He had some conversation with Mr. Truscott during the meal. The identification is made absolute by the fact that Mr. Truscott was arrested in the presence, and to the astonishment, of Mr. Higham.

"In the interests of justice, Mr. Higham will give evidence as to the time of arrival of Mr. Truscott. He is also prepared to state, if required, that there was nothing in his demeanour or conversation to suggest that he came from the commission of a fratricidal crime. He remarked to the headwaiter, immediately after Mr. Truscott's arrest, that he must be either a very cold-blooded criminal or an innocent man."

Mr. Leslie Tonks recognised efficiency, in whatever garb it might come before him. He said: "That is good work. Send me a written copy of your report. The next thing I want you to do is to get into conversation with the porter whose duty it is to clear up the offices when the staff of Truscott & Rowton go out to lunch. Get him to talk, if you can, about the murder, particularly of what he saw and heard, and let me have it as exactly as possible. Note down what you can, especially anything which would tend to throw doubt on whether Roger Truscott must have committed the crime. If you get anything definite, I may want you to give evidence that the words were spoken."

He dismissed the man, feeling that another step, however short, had been taken toward the elucidation of the mystery. But he recognised that he had not even approached the solution of the central problem.

He strolled into the office of the senior partner, feeling a need to tell someone what he had done, and to obtain the judgement of another mind. He found Mr. Weatherhead ready to listen, and disposed to approve his efforts.

He was discomfited for a moment, after he had gone with particularity into the proofs that now existed of the time of Roger's leaving and of the calling of the police, when Mr. Weatherhead said: "Excellent. But you haven't told me yet what you're hoping to prove. Is it that Roger hadn't had time to commit the crime, or that there was time for someone else to have done it as well?"

Until he saw that the two things were not antipathetical.

Then he said: "I'm hoping to prove that someone else could have had time to do it, but of course if I could show that Roger hadn't, it would be a double weight in the same scale; but I should say that's impossible. It wouldn't take seconds to fire a shot, and throw down the gun."

"No. I don't see how you could prove that. The other's more possible, though it won't take you far."

"As a fact, I was trying to test a bit more than that. The tale is that the police were called in immediately that the shot was fired, and the body discovered. How long would that take? If the interval between Roger going and the calling of the police is too long, then something else must have happened."

"Yes. It's a good point. The trouble is to see how you can urge it without attacking the good faith of three independent witnesses."

"Yes. And it may be necessary to do that."

Mr. Weatherhead did not deny the necessity, but he looked troubled. He said: "If you do that and fail, you throw away his last chance."

That had been clear to Leslie from the first. The accusation could not be met with blank denial and the pleading of extenuating circumstances at the same time. If a jury ultimately credited the account of the three witnesses in the upper room, it would have done no good to attack their veracity. It might be regarded as an insolently foolish attempt to deny an evident, shameless crime. But he had chosen his path, and saw that it must be walked boldly, if at all.

"That," he said, with all the confidence he could put into his voice, "is just why we mustn't fail."

They went into calculation of time, at their extreme and narrowest limits.

At the end, Mr. Weatherhead would say no more than: "Well, it's a fine point. You'd want a good counsel to shake a jury on that. Who are you proposing to have?"

"I've scarcely thought of that yet. Roger says he leaves it entirely to us." He added, with some hesitation: "I wasn't sure that I shouldn't like the chance of questioning those witnesses myself before the committal."

Mr. Weatherhead did not discourage this. He said: "You must decide that for yourself. I've known it to answer well at times when the solicitor puts on the gloves for the first round. The danger is that he may be tempted to talk too much. It's natural enough to want to score all the points himself instead of putting them in the brief for the other man. Have you thought that it may be best to reserve the defence entirely?"

"Yes. I've thought of that, if I'm no more advanced than I am now. But I'm not sure even then. If they're telling lies, it's no help to them to have to tell them twice over, six weeks apart."

"Well," his partner repeated, "I shall leave it to you."

He saw that the real trouble was that they had no proof that anyone had been telling lies, or intended to do so.

CHAPTER XIV.

THE remainder of the week passed in an unceasing activity of enquiry, both on the part of Roger Truscott's official enemies and professional friends, but the results were of too negative a character to require more than the briefest record.

On Thursday morning Mr. Rowton rang up Mr. Tonks and said, "I expect you've made young Truscott see sense this time?" And Leslie replied: "If you mean have we persuaded him to sign the deed, I'm afraid not. His mind's made up about that, and we shall just have to drop the idea." He thought he heard a muttered curse, which would have seemed inconsistent with the attitude which Mr. Rowton had declared at their last interview, but, if so, it was instantly suppressed. The answer that followed had a tone of indifferent and somewhat sarcastic finality: "Well, it's his funeral, not ours," and, with those words, Mr. Rowton rang off.

Leslie Tonks, reading a sinister meaning which Mr. Rowton may not have meant into what was no more than a conventional metaphor, was roused to a sudden anger, and realisation that the speaker was a man he had never liked nor entirely trusted. But he recognised that there is a wide difference between distrusting a man in his business dealings, and regarding him as capable of giving false evidence which must be designed to hang an innocent man. Besides—if Roger had not shot his brother, who had? And even in business matters, Leslie might be disposed to distrust a man he disliked, as we all are, but he must recognise that his business record was one of success and established reputation.

After this little telephone skirmish, the week passed without further reference to the sale of the business, or its future destiny, either from its auditor or managing director. Leslie gave the matter no further thought, being sufficiently occupied in raking the debris of past events for jewels of evidence which were not there.

Enquiries, intensively pursued, into Cyril's college occupations and acquaintances, and particularly into the events of his last night in London, though the last had proved to be of a particularly unsavoury character, had failed to discover that he had been involved in any quarrel, or that he was blackmailed, or indebted to moneylenders or gambling houses, or that any motive of feminine jealousy might supply a possible assassin, if not an explanation of the crime.

He had been only in his twentieth year, and though he had been knocking with some energy at the gates of vice, he did not appear to have gone far enough to encounter any of the ultimate consequences with which it can be relied upon to reward its worshippers.

The police, pursuing parallel enquiries with a different purpose, had failed to find any previous cause of quarrel between the brothers, such as Inspector Byfleet would have regarded as making his case complete. Indeed, some letters from Roger which were found in the rooms of the dead youth, were of such a character, in their evidences of good-humoured, though protesting, support of the extravagance of the younger brother, as to give the Inspector a moment's uneasy doubt as to whether, after all, there might be no element of disturbing doubt in a case that seemed so simple and sure. But he went over the facts again, and he saw that there was only one conclusion to which they pointed with irresistible force.

Cyril had quarrelled with Roger, and no one else, and Roger, and no one else, had been behind him when he was shot on the stairs. The Inspector observed the baffling enigma of human conduct, as must be the frequent reflection of those who deal with the detection and suppression of crime. The secret antipathy, the growing grudge (had Roger hated his brother more deeply every time he wrote one of those careless, friendly, protesting notes, enclosing another of the frequent cheques which must have made so large a reduction in his own resources?), the smouldering antipathy which so small a spark might start to a fatal flare! Doubtless, this stubborn opposition to Roger's equal though quieter determination to continue the business—this outcry that would not cease, and took at last a tone of half-drunken threats—had been that fatal spark, the last intolerable straw.

An examination of the banking account of the dead youth had been equally fruitless. There were not even any payments to moneylenders, nor did he appear to have bet more than occasionally, and for comparatively moderate amounts. On enquiry being made upon the betting gentleman with the Scottish name and the Hebrew nose with whom he had a credit account, it was found that any balances against himself had been readily and promptly settled, and the account was actually balanced at the time of the tragedy. Debts there certainly were, but nothing of a vexatious or excessive appearance.

It seemed that his brother's chequebook had supported his own liberal allowance sufficiently to prevent any acute financial crisis arising. Finding nothing that threw any light on the murder in any way, Inspector Byfleet was confirmed in the belief that its cause must lie in the quarrel with his brother which had immediately preceded the murder. Negatively, he had strengthened his case by the elimination of more remote possibilities.

Enquiries respecting the revolver had proved equally fruitless. On every side, the case appeared to resist the attempt to complicate its severe and obvious simplicity. It remained static: a problem which would not alter its factors for any irritation on the part of those who were dissatisfied with the solution themselves suggested. It appeared useless to consider that there might be other pieces which should be seen on the board.

So the days passed.

CHAPTER XV.

ROGER TRUSCOTT took his place in the dock, the centre of many curious and few friendly eyes, feeling in better health and much better spirits than may be considered natural to a man who had spent a week in lonely confinement, and was now charged with the commission of brutal and cowardly murder.

But there was some satisfaction in feeling that the time of waiting was over, and that of action had come, there was some mental stimulus in the fact that the accusation was at last to be formulated, under oath, and subject to the scrutiny of a presumably impartial magistrate and his own legal allies.

The stipendiary magistrate, Mr. Buxted, K.C., would have been a much surprised man had anyone questioned his impartiality. He was reputed to be fair to the point of scrupulosity toward those who were charged before him within the limit of his authority, and such a reputation is not won without being well deserved. But in a case such as that with which he was now to deal, in which the authority of the Home Office was behind the indictment, he regarded his normal duty as being no more than to oversee that the case would be properly presented for trial by a higher court. He was not conscious of this, and would have resented its specific statement. The authority of the police has advanced with such quiet regularity, during the century of their existence, that the magistracy have been scarcely conscious of the extent to which they have become subordinated. Mr. Buxted, his outward dignity secure without necessity for self-assertion in the deferential atmosphere which surrounded him, regarded the prisoner, before he had listened to a single witness against him, as one whom it would be his part to commit for trial to the Central Criminal Court.

He looked at Mr. Wedland-Wedland, a K.C. like himself (but making about five times his own income), who had been briefed by the Crown, and asked: "Shall you be able to finish your case today,

Mr. Wedland-Wedland, or do you think there will be occasion for a further adjournment?"

The learned counsel said that he anticipated no difficulty. "It is," he said, "really quite simple, and I shall not have to trouble you with more than six witnesses."

Mr. Buxted replied that, as Mr. Wedland-Wedland was now ready to complete the case, it might be convenient to go on with it tomorrow, if the day's sitting should prove too short. He had, in fact, reserved the two days in anticipation of a position of which he had already been unofficially notified.

Mr. Wedland-Wedland said it would be convenient to him.

Mr. Buxted, with his habitual courtesy, looked to the solicitor who was appearing for the prisoner, to ask: "And for you, Mr. Tonks?"—but the question was of little more than a perfunctory character. Leslie, who would have preferred another week's adjournment after the principal witnesses for the prosecution had told their tales, made no demur.

He saw that the fact that he had not briefed counsel at this stage must make it appear (which might have seemed probable in any event) that he had advised his client to reserve such defence as he might be able to make, so that the issue would not be fought out until it came before the higher tribunal. But as his position was still that of a boxer who strives to prolong defence while waiting for his opponent's error, he was careful to say nothing by which this impression might be disturbed.

Mr. Wedland-Wedland rose to open his case with the easy feeling that he had no complication to fear, and little opposition to face.

He was a ponderous man, with a wide expanse of face, in which a large fleshy nose had a beak-like prominence—an effect which was increased by the high black arches which hooded two owl-like eyes. He was a sound lawyer, slow and solid in all he did. When he addressed a jury he could be heavily persuasive, and would sometimes attempt to win them to a good-humoured intimacy with an elephantine joke. He had a habit of dangling some gold-rimmed eye-glasses in his left hand unceasingly as he spoke. If the steady flow of his eloquence should fail, he would adjust these glasses elaborately on his nose, as though they were necessary to enable him to make reference to his brief, but this was regarded as no more than a trick of habit by those who observed that he appeared able to read it without assistance at other times.

He had for his junior a Mr. Bayley Atkinson, young barrister who was in process of learning that wealthy and influential friends, and many relationships in the legal profession, may provide opportunities, but cannot manufacture a successful advocate. In fact, the legal talent which had been engaged for the Crown was indicative of the judgement of its solicitors that the case require no more than to be presented in a solid common sense way, it having no complexity commensurate to the public interest that had been excited by the social position of the dead and living protagonist in this fratricidal crime.

Mr. Wedland-Wedland's opening statement was brief and lucid. He knew that he was not addressing a jury, and he confined himself to such an outline of the case as would enable Mr. Buxted to appreciate the points which the various witnesses would be called to prove. It would add little to what has been set out already, and that little can best be heard from the mouths of the witnesses themselves. Mr. Wedland-Wedland, having opened his case, put Inspector Byfleet into the box. After the usual preliminaries, the examination proceeded:

"I believe, Inspector Byfleet, that, at about a quarter or twenty past one P.M. on Wednesday, the 12th of this month, you were at an address in Cannon Street—on a matter which has no relation to the present case—when you were rung up from Scotland Yard, and instructed to proceed at once to the premises of Truscott & Rowton, Ltd., in Cannon Street, to investigate a report that a man had been shot there?"

"Yes."

"And you went at once?"

"Yes."

"What did you find?"

"I was received by the managing director, Mr. Rowton, who showed me the body of a young man, which he identified as that of Cyril Truscott, lying at the foot of a flight of stairs which descend to a side street from the private offices of the firm, which are on the second floor of the building."

"He was dead?"

"Yes. Obviously."

"Was there anything, apart from the condition of the body, to indicate how he had died?"

"There was a revolver lying close to the wall on the fourth stair from the top."

"Is this the weapon?"

The revolver was handed up to Inspector Byfleet, and identified by him.

"In what condition was it?"

"Five chambers were loaded, and one had been discharged."

"Did you make any other observations?"

"I observed a trace of blood on the sixth stair from the top."

"The stairs are of stone?"

"Yes. A long straight flight, and rather steep."

"So that, if a man were shot at the top he would fall headlong the whole way to the foot?"

"Yes."

"Was the street door open or shut?"

"It was shut."

"Will it open from the outside?"

"Only by the use of a key. It is fastened on the inside with a Yale lock."

"But it could have been readily opened from the inside?"

"Yes."

"Was there any other access to the stairs, except the door at the head, and that which opened to the street?"

"There was a locked door halfway down, where there is a small landing at the side of the stairs. It had obviously not been opened for a long time—probably years."

"It was subsequently opened in your presence?"

"Yes. We opened it with great difficulty. It had swollen somewhat, and the hinges had become stiff."

"It would not have been possible for who ever may have shot Cyril Truscott to have come through that door, or escaped by it?"

"No. The idea would be absurd."

"What conclusion did you draw from the position of the body and the injuries it had received?"

"I thought that murder had been committed."

"You concluded at once that it could not be a case of suicide?"

"Yes. He had been shot in the back."

"And you naturally made enquiries as to who could have committed the crime?"

"Yes. I took statements from Mr. Rowton, and from a clerk named Albert Menzies, and from Alfred Bellman, the porter."

"And as a result of what you were told—I am not asking you to say what it was, which we shall have from those witnesses themselves—but as a result of those statements you resolved upon the arrest of Roger Truscott, the brother of the dead man?"

"Yes."

"You did, in fact, arrest him within the hour at the Brading Restaurant?"

"Yes."

"Thank you, Inspector Byfleet. That will do."

Mr. Wedland-Wedland sat down.

Mr. Buxted, who had been taking careful notes of this evidence, paused with a lifted pen: "Any questions, Mr. Tonks?"

Leslie rose with a feeling that he must make every brick he could, let the straw be as short as it might, though there was little here that he hoped to gain.

"You have said that it was a quarter or twenty past one when you were first notified of this murder by Scotland Yard?"

Mr. Wedland-Wedland raised his owl-like eyebrows at the form in which this question was put, and Mr. Buxted rubbed his chin in a meditative way. An inexperienced young solicitor! It seemed hardly fair to the prisoner, though, of course, it could make no difference in the end. The fact that it was obviously murder was no reason that the word should come from the mouth of the prisoner's own advocate.

But Leslie knew that the line of defence to which he was committed would allow no opportunity for palliation of the crime, even if there were any hope of ultimately obtaining a modified verdict or a recommendation to mercy under any circumstances. And that being so, the more he allowed the monstrous nature of such a death from a brother's hand to be thrown into bold relief, the stronger would be his argument that Roger was not of the disposition to have committed so base a crime.

He disregarded, if he observed, the way in which his question was received by his legal protagonists, hearing only the Inspector's answering "Yes."

"You cannot say more exactly?"

"No."

"But the exact time when the call at Scotland Yard was received will be on record?"

"Yes."

"Will you obtain it for me?"

"Yes."

"You regard that as a point of importance, Mr. Tonks?" the magistrate asked.

"I think it may be. It is at least a point on which we should be quite clear."

Mr. Buxted agreed about that. He knew the importance of having the depositions complete to the satisfaction of the High Court Judge who would ultimately preside over the trial. He had been publicly rebuked some years before for an omission for which he had had little responsibility, and it was a humiliation he would never forget.

"You had better"—he addressed Inspector Byfleet—"have a witness here this afternoon who can prove that point."

Leslie Tonks went on: "You are satisfied that Cyril Truscott was shot with the revolver now produced?"

"Yes."

"Have you been able to trace its ownership?"

"No."

"You cannot say that it has ever been in the prisoner's possession?"

"No."

"Nor that he ever possessed any firearm of any description?"

"No."

"Nor that he has ever been known to use one?"

"No."

"Were there any finger-marks upon it?"

"No."

"What do you conclude from that?"

"It must have been deliberately wiped after being used, or perhaps used with a gloved hand."

"It would take some moments to wipe it after the shot had been fired?"

"A few seconds."

"Had Roger Truscott any gloves with him when he was arrested?"

"Not to my knowledge."

"What was his demeanour when you arrested him?"

"He seemed surprised."

"Astonished?"

"Yes. You may say that."

"He protested his innocence?"

"He said that he was entirely ignorant of the fact that his brother had been shot."

"Thank you, Inspector, that is all."

Mr. Wedland-Wedland rose ponderously: "One moment, Inspector. It does not necessarily follow, if the revolver were not wiped after the shot was fired, that the murderer must have worn gloves? He might have held the weapon in a handkerchief when he fired?"

"Yes, of course."

"Quite so. When you make arrests, for whatever offences against the law, is it unusual for accused persons to protest their innocence?"

"No."

"It is a very common experience?"

"Yes."

"Particularly when they have reason to fear arrest beforehand, and time to consider what it will be best to say at that moment?"

"Yes."

Inspector Byfleet, having given his evidence fairly to both sides, was allowed to step down.

Mr. Wedland-Wedland now asked permission to call Sir Lionel Tipshift. The famous Government expert was in court, and his time was more precious than that of ordinary mortals. The expected assent having been obtained, Sir Lionel stepped into the box, took the oath in a formally perfunctory manner, as one who submitted to a slightly derogatory proceeding as an example to lesser men, and gave the result of the autopsy at which he had presided. Stripped of the inevitable jargon of his profession, it stated that the bullet, which must have been fired from a distance of not less than two feet, had entered on the left side of the spine, which it narrowly missed, penetrated the left lung in a somewhat downward direction, and passed through the left ventricle of the heart, finally being flattened against one of the lower ribs, which it fractured.

Beside that, the dead man had a broken neck, and other fractures and injuries, all of which were minutely described.

"And the cause of death, Sir Lionel, in your opinion?"

"It is impossible to say that with certainty. There were two injuries, either of which would have been almost instantly fatal."

"Then the first may be logically preferred as the cause of death?"

"I cannot go quite that far. The second—the injuries being as severe as they were—might be slightly the more instantaneously fatal. It is impossible to say with certainty."

"The injuries, other than the bullet wound, might all have been caused by the fall?"

"Yes, there is no reasonable doubt that they were. The body probably turned over completely more than once in the course of the fall. It alighted upon its head, in such a position that the neck was broken with the whole weight of the body as it fell over."

"But you can say definitely that Cyril Truscott was fatally wounded before he fell?"

"Yes."

"And it was that injury—the bullet wound—which caused his collapse and fall?"

"It is a reasonable presumption."

"That is all, thank you, Sir Lionel."

"Any questions, Mr. Tonks?" Mr. Buxted asked.

"Just one or two. Sir Lionel, when Cyril Truscott was shot he must have been almost at the top of the stairs?"

"Yes. I should say he was."

"Not lower than the fourth step?"

"Probably not, there having been blood on the sixth."

"You conclude that he collapsed on to the sixth, and then turned head-over-heels as he fell the whole length of the flight?"

"That is almost certainly what occurred."

"The bullet went straight through from back to front?"

"Yes."

"He could not have been turning round, or looking backward up the stairs, when he was shot?"

"It is highly improbable."

"I ask you to place it higher than that—that it is impossible."

"He might have been turning his head."

"But not more?"

"No. I should say not."

"And anyone following him, and shooting when he was only on the fourth stair, must have done so instantly that the door had closed behind them?"

"Yes. That appears reasonable."

"With scarcely time to draw a concealed weapon, and wrap a handkerchief round it?"

Mr. Wedland-Wedland rose. "I must object to this cross-examination. The witness is being asked to theorise on matters which are outside his profession."

Mr. Buxted said: "I am afraid I cannot allow that last question, Mr. Tonks."

"I was only trying to establish that, if Cyril Truscott was shot in the manner the witness had described—from which I do not dissent—it must have been a deliberate murder, previously planned."

"That is a matter of opinion on which Sir Lionel cannot give evidence."

Leslie said he must bow to the magistrate's ruling. He felt that he had gained as much as though he had obtained a reply.

The arched eyebrows of the prosecuting counsel were raised again. He muttered to his colleague: "Planned by whom, except the man who followed him through the door?"

Mr. Bayley-Atkinson replied: "It looks as though he's going to argue that there must have been a conspiracy, and Truscott's only one of a gang."

Mr. Wedland-Wedland's experienced opinion that the prisoner's solicitor was a very foolish young man, did not enable him to go that far. He saw that such a suggestion, unless it should be supported by some evidence entirely beyond his own horizon, was fantastic in its improbability, and it was not a line of defence which could do Roger Truscott any possible good. To shoot a brother in the back on a sudden angry impulse is bad enough, and is not improved by the fact that you have a weapon at hand and already prepared for use, but it is still worse if it can be shown that you have acted on a settled purpose deliberately planned with others beforehand.

No, he was sure that Mr. Tonks would not be quite so foolish as to be leading up to such a position, but he recognised that there was some force in the argument, from whatever motive it came. He hastily turned the pages of his brief as he spoke. Yes. It was sudden impulse he had been instructed to urge. He scrawled a hasty note on the margin.

Mr. Buxted was speaking: "Will your next witness take very long, Mr. Wedland-Wedland?"

Counsel glanced at the clock, and understood the point of the question.

"I have one," he answered, "who will not take long, and who might conveniently be taken now." He called Mr. William Siskin.

Mr. Siskin entered the box briskly. He was a small, yellow-haired man, with an abrupt, birdlike quality which suggested that some similar ancestor might have earned the family name. He had a manner which was nervous and yet pertly assured.

He recounted how he had seen the prisoner leave by the street-door. He did not know his name, but he identified him as the man he saw in the dock. He was quite certain of that. He had served him with cigarettes on several occasions during the previous week. He had a good memory for faces. The time was about 1:05 P.M. He could say that with certainty, as he had a train to catch at Cannon Street Station at 1:10. Would he remember if he missed it? Yes. He certainly should. He had not missed his train once in the last five years. His assistant went out for his own lunch at 12:25, and had to be back at one. Then he left himself.

On this occasion he had been standing at the door giving his assistant a parting instruction about some reserve stock which was to be got out, when he noticed the prisoner leave through the door which was next his own. No, he had heard no shot. He did not suppose he would have noticed it if he had, unless it had been quite loud. Cannon Street is not a quiet thoroughfare.

Mr. Tonks rose to cross-examine.

"You say you never miss your train, Mr. Siskin?"

"No, I don't ever."

"Your assistant must be very punctual in his return?"

"Yes, he knows better than to be late."

"I am sure he does. Probably he allows himself a minute or two on the right side?"

"I daresay he does."

"And when he comes in you take it as a signal to go?"

"Yes."

"So that it might be a minute or two earlier than 1:05, rather than later, when you saw Mr. Truscott go out? Shall we say that it would not be later than 1:04 P.M.?"

"It might have been about that."

"Mr. Truscott did not leave hurriedly, or appear in any way disturbed in manner?"

"I didn't notice anything."

"But you would have noticed if he had? You have told us that you are an observant man."

"Yes, I expect I should."

"In fact, Mr. Truscott said good-day to you as he passed, and that may have helped you to remember having seen him leave?"

"Yes, I think he did."

"You recall that, now that I mention it?"

"Yes, he did speak as he passed. I remember now."

"And his manner was just as quiet and natural as it always is, or you would have noticed the difference, and naturally have informed the police when you were questioned about the incident?"

"Yes, I didn't notice anything out of the ordinary."

Mr. Tonks sat down, and the prosecution had no further questions to ask.

Mr. Buxted said that the court would adjourn for forty minutes.

Mr. Wedland-Wedland saw the line of defence which Mr. Tonks had decided to take. Absolute innocence! Perhaps the best he could do, but how absurd, how futile, in view of the evidence which he would bring forward that afternoon. Probably Mr. Tonks did not know how damning, how devastating, that evidence would prove to be.

Mr. Weatherhead, who had let his own work go, that he might watch the trial of the son of an old-time friend, had sat gravely silent and observant, giving no sign of his thoughts as the morning passed. As they went out together, he cheered his partner with a word of praise, though of less hope.

"You've done well this morning. I couldn't see that you missed anything. But the stiff fences are still ahead."

CHAPTER XVI.

MR. ROWTON entered the witness box. He had the aspect of a man who comes reluctantly to a distasteful task, and is not accustomed to doing that against which his temper rebels. He had the flushed face of a man who had lunched too well.

He went through the formality of the oath, and answered the necessary preliminary questions in a clear, curt tone which could be heard in all parts of the crowded court. It could be noticed that Mr. Wedland-Wedland addressed him in a manner slightly more courteous, if not more deferential, than that which he had thought suitable for the previous witness. Mr. Rowton was the head of a city firm of a worldwide repute and unblemished reputation, and deserved some sympathy for being involved in the events which had brought him there.

But though Leslie had thought to watch and weigh every word which might come from the witnesses of the afternoon, these preliminary questions passed him unheard, and it was with a difficult effort of mental adjustment that he was subsequently able to bring himself back to the urgent duty of listening to Mr. Rowton's account of the events of the fatal morning, as they were narrated under the skilful guidance of the counsel for the prosecution.

For just as Leslie had taken his place, a friendly solicitor had leaned over from the seats behind him, touching his arm and passing over the midday edition of a financial paper.

Following his pointing finger, Leslie's eyes fell on a paragraph head. "Sharp fall in L. & R.'s this morning." Under this caption there was a short paragraph:

> A sharp fall of nearly seven points in Lessing & Rivermouth's shares occurred when the Exchange opened this morning, following reports, which appear to be well authenticated, that a contract, the value of which is estimated at between £2,000,000 and

£3,000,000, spread over the next six years, has been secured by the rival firm of Truscott & Rowton, from the Brazilian Government. It is stated that the Truscott & Rowton tender was substantially the higher of the two, and it had been assumed in commercial circles that L. & R. would secure the contract. But the Brazilian Government appear to have been influenced by the high reputation of the older firm, and its past experience of similar work in the Southern Continent. (Truscott & Rowton is a private company, and its shares are not quoted on the exchange.)

That was all. There was no allusion to the fact that one of the heads of the firm of Truscott & Rowton would be giving evidence that afternoon against a colleague who was also its principal shareholder, and who now stood in the dock on a charge of fratricidal crime, though there could be no doubt that these events were in the mind of whoever had written it, as they were familiar to every newspaper reader throughout the land. The report itself might be no more than one of those baseless rumours which are set afloat for speculative purposes. It might be denied in the next hour. But to Leslie, looking desperately round for the straw which his brick-making so sadly lacked, it seemed like the small cloud that told of a coming rain in Elijah's sky.

If it were true, Roger's judgement or instinct had been right in refusing to sell. But had Rowton known, or had good cause to suspect? And, in any event, what connection could it have with the present tragedy? Had it been Roger who died, a sufficient effort of imagination might have made Rowton his murderer, though Leslie's knowledge of men was sufficient to dismiss that possibility very easily. Rowton was not of the kind who murder those who oppose them. His battles were fought with other weapons on different ground. But he had had a quarrel with Roger—a quarrel which, it now appeared, might have had more at stake than could have been previously supposed. With Cyril he had none. Cyril was on his side. He had been urging his brother to sell. He would doubtless have continued to do so. The idea was silly. And yet there was something here to be followed up, and who knew to what it might lead at last? But, for the moment, he must put it out of his mind. What was Rowton saying now?

"Yes. It was the first time I had seen him. I believe he may have come to the office during the previous week, but we did not meet."

"How long had he been there?"

"About two hours."

"That means that they had come in at about eleven?"

"Cyril Truscott came in about that time. Roger had come in much earlier."

"What were their relations during the morning?"

"They were quarrelling."

"All the time?"

"Practically so. They came into my own room at one time, and I tried to get them to agree, but it was no use."

"What was the cause of the quarrel?"

"It was a business matter. Roger had charge of his brother's estate during his minority, and he declined to regard Cyril's wishes respecting it."

"Roger had only come of age during the previous fortnight?"

"I believe that is so."

"And Cyril was a year or two younger?"

"So it appeared."

"So that there was little difference between the brothers in point of age, but Roger's seniority gave him entire control over his brother's property, as well as his own?"

"That was what I understood the position to be."

"And having that legal advantage, Roger was proposing to exercise it without reference to his brother's wishes, and, indeed, in direct opposition to them?"

"Yes."

"And this quarrel continued until the arrival of the luncheon hour?"

"Yes."

"Did it diminish or increase in violence?"

"It was particularly violent in the last few minutes."

"And how did it terminate, as far as your own observation went?"

"I was standing at the door of my own room. I was on my way out to lunch. It was a few minutes after one, and most of the staff had already left. I was detained by Menzies, one of the departmental heads, who had come to make a report to me which I had asked to have before I left.

"As we were speaking, Roger and Cyril came out of the adjoining room, which was Roger's office. Cyril was in advance. There were some angry words, and a scuffle at the door of the room. I think Roger was trying to push past, and Cyril held him back for something he was determined to say. Cyril was a good deal the bigger and stronger of the two."

The remark caused many eyes to be turned to the prisoner, sitting in the dock, listening to this evidence with outward self-control, but a concentrated watchfulness that showed the tenseness of his restraint.

The witness went on. "Then Cyril pushed Roger back, and shouted something about being sick or fed-up, and went toward the door that opens on to the stairs. As he crossed the floor of the outer office, he shouted over his shoulder that he was coming back in the afternoon, and not going till he got his own way. Then he went out.

"Roger stood for a moment at the door of his room, and then followed him quickly. He went out of the door to the stairs, almost as it closed behind Cyril."

He paused, as though reluctant to give words to the fatal sequence of the long quarrel that he had described, with what most of his hearers thought to be a deliberate moderation, and yet with clear and businesslike brevity.

"And then, Mr. Rowton?" Counsel's voice, on its most suavely persuasive note, sounded to the limits of the silent court.

"After that, almost instantly, there was a loud report from the stairs. Menzies said, 'What on earth's that?' and ran to the door. When he looked through, he called out, and I went to him. Bellman came up a moment later. We saw Cyril Truscott lying at the foot of the stairs.

"We went down, and saw that he was dead. As we descended, there was a pistol lying on the stairs by the wall. I said that it would be best to touch nothing and call up the police."

"And that was done?"

"Yes, Menzies phoned at once."

"And nothing was touched till Inspector Byfleet arrived?"

"No."

"You know nothing beyond what you have told the Court regarding this tragedy, or the circumstances leading thereto?"

"Not except what I have heard from others."

"Thank you, Mr. Rowton."

Mr. Wedland-Wedland sat down, making a gesture to Mr. Tonks which might be interpreted to mean: "Your witness now, at your own risk!" And Mr. Tonks accepting the challenge, rose to cross-examine.

"I am sure you realise, Mr. Rowton, that this is a very serious matter."

"Yes. Obviously."

"And you would wish to be correspondingly careful that your evidence should be fair and full, neither making any inaccurate statement, nor omitting anything which may be material to the defence?"

"Yes. Certainly."

"Recalling the evidence that you have just given, are you prepared to swear deliberately that those standards have been observed?"

"I don't know what you mean?"

"It is a simple question."

"I have naturally endeavoured to be as accurate as possible."

"I wish to be quite fair to you, Mr. Rowton. I propose to ask the permission of the Court that your evidence, in particular so far as it relates to the events of the 12th inst., shall be read over; after which I shall repeat the question I have asked already."

"And which," Mr. Wedland-Wedland interjected, "has been answered already."

He rose as he spoke and addressed Mr. Buxted as he went on: "I am reluctant to interpose, but the witness has answered the question once, and I submit that Mr. Tonks must accept his reply."

"On what ground do you object to his memory being refreshed," Leslie enquired, "by his evidence being read over to him?"

Before the prosecuting counsel could reply, Mr. Buxted spoke: "If there be something in the witness's evidence which you have reason to think may be inaccurate, Mr. Tonks, could you not be more specific?"

"No," Leslie replied, after a moment's consideration. "I am afraid not. But I can assure you that I make this request with a full sense of responsibility. I would point out that the case against my client, as I understand it, at present rests entirely upon the course of events which occurred during a short time after 1:00 P.M., and it is of vital moment that these facts should be accurately ascertained. What I ask is that Mr. Rowton's evidence, as far as it relates to the events of that day, should be read over to him, and that he should be given an opportunity of amplifying or amending it in any particular in which he may observe that it may otherwise tend to mislead the Court."

Mr. Buxted sat back, and was not quick to reply. His fingers tapped on the desk. The request was somewhat unusual, and it appeared to be one which should be refused. But, on the other hand, if he should give his consent, it was hard to see that any failure of justice could follow, or that the prosecution would have valid ground of complaint. A truthful witness could have no objection to confirming the evidence which he had given within the last hour; an untruthful or inaccurate one should not complain of an opportunity of correcting any error he might have made.

On the other hand, if some point of vital importance might ultimately hinge upon this request, he did not wish to run any risk, however slight, of a repetition of that experience of earlier years.

Apart from that—and it may have been the decisive consideration—he wished to be fair to the defence. While it did not occur to him to doubt that it would be his duty to commit the prisoner for trial, he wished the preliminary hearing which he controlled to be scrupulously fair in the presentation of the case to the higher tribunal before which it must go.

"The request," he said at last, "is somewhat unusual, but it has been made, and in view of the gravity of the issues at stake, I do not feel it to be one that I should refuse. Mr. Stringer, I shall be glad if you will read over your notes of this witness's evidence, as far as they relate to the events of the 12th inst."

Mr. Wedland-Wedland made no further objection, and the shorthand writer read out the evidence, while Mr. Rowton, finding some difficulty in maintaining the demeanour which he felt the situation demanded, was accommodated, on Mr. Buxted's instructions, with a seat in the witness box.

The reader's voice ceased, and Mr. Tonks rose at once: "You have heard your evidence read over, Mr. Rowton. Is there anything you desire to add?"

"No. I don't know that there is. Of course, I'm here to answer any questions I can."

"There are a few that I shall have to ask you. But regarding the evidence you have already given, is there anything you desire to amend?"

"No, it sounded correct to me."

"Very well, I accept that. We heard evidence this morning that Mr. Roger Truscott must have left not later than five minutes after one, and perhaps slightly earlier. I am not questioning that. Do you agree?"

"It was after the clerks had left."

"But not much?"

"No. I daresay you would be right about that."

"I will tell you what I propose to submit to the Court, when, in due course, I shall ask for this case to be dismissed—that it will have been proved by the prosecution itself, and by another witness whom I shall call, that Roger Truscott left at four minutes past one. Now you have sworn and confirmed that the shot that killed his brother was fired immediately that he went out to the stairs, that you and others went at once to the discovery of his brother's body, and that Menzies telephoned Scotland Yard immediately afterwards. Will you tell the Court at what time that call should have been received?"

As Leslie asked this question, he was conscious that he had not only startled the presiding magistrate and the counsel for the prosecution to an equal amazement, he had ruined his own reputation, and probably assured that his client's life would end in the hangman's shed, if the event should show that he had bluffed too high. He took what consolation he could from observing that Mr. Rowton's confident demeanour had given way to puzzled discomfiture which his business training was not able to more than partially cover.

"I suppose," he answered, "that it was ten minutes or a quarter past."

"Which?"

"I couldn't say exactly. I didn't think about it."

"But you can recollect the course of events. You have sworn to them. You can estimate how long or rather how short a time they would have required."

Mr. Wedland-Wedland rose again: "I submit that it is no part of the duty of the witness to make such calculation. He has given the facts as he recalls them. As to the exact minutes at which the police were summoned, he has sworn that he cannot say more definitely than that it was between ten and a quarter minutes past one."

"I would remind you, Mr. Tonks," Mr. Buxted said, "that the point, of whatever importance it may be, which I am not yet in a position to judge, fortunately does not depend upon the memory of this witness. As you know, I have already requested the presence of a witness by whom it may be formally proved."

"Then I will leave it there," Leslie replied, fearing that to press the witness further, at that stage, might do more harm by forfeiting the sympathy of the court than would be compensated by any admission he was likely to get. He was watching the moving hands of the clock with some apprehension also. It might be of vital importance to have the two other witnesses—Menzies and Bellman, who were now waiting outside the court, and unable to hear what was said—examined that afternoon, before they would be able to discuss, or the prosecution consider, the inferences of the question which he had raised.

But there was one other point on which he could not afford to let Mr. Rowton go free.

"You have mentioned that there was some difference between Roger and his brother on financial matters. I suggest to you that you have greatly exaggerated its character?"

"I have only told what I saw and heard."

"And that any boyish violence of conduct or language there may have been was entirely on the part of the younger brother?"

The witness was less quick to reply to that question. "He did most of the shouting," he said at last. "I can't go beyond that."

"And I suggest further that this quarrel, such as it was, would be an utterly inadequate motive for such a murder, and that the two matters have not the slightest connection with one another?"

Mr. Wedland-Wedland was on his feet immediately.

"I object," he said. "How can the witness possibly answer that? He has given evidence that he heard a quarrel, that he heard a shot, and that he then discovered the dead body of Cyril Truscott after his brother had been with him a moment before. How in reason can he be asked to swear that these events are in no way connected? I submit that the question is inadmissible on other grounds, which are too obvious for it to be necessary for me to urge them."

Mr. Buxted smiled upon Mr. Tonks: "You know," he said, "I cannot possibly allow that."

Mr. Tonks showed no annoyance in his reply. He was aiming, if he could not shake his evidence otherwise, to show Mr. Rowton as a hostile rather than an impartial witness, and the point of this examination was still to come.

"I must withdraw the question," he said easily. "You were aware, Mr. Rowton, of the subject of this difference—of this quarrel, if you will?"

"Yes."

"Thoroughly familiar with it?"

"I knew what it was about."

"Did you think that the position taken up by Roger Truscott was wise and right in his brother's interest?"

"No. I can't say I did."

"Do you think so now?"

"No. I don't."

"Really?"

Mr. Rowton remained silent. He appeared to resent the question, and may have felt that he would reasonably object to being asked it a second time.

"Then, in view of that reply, I must ask you to state specifically what that difference was."

"I don't see what that has to do with the matter."

"Perhaps not. But I must still ask you to answer the question."

"I have already explained that it was in relation to the realisation of Cyril Truscott's inheritance."

"I ask you to be more specific in explanation."

The witness glanced at Mr. Wedland-Wedland, as though for his assistance in an awkward position, but that gentleman, though obviously on the alert, apparently felt unable to intervene.

"I don't think I can be more specific without possible detriment to business interests which have nothing to do with this case."

"Even if that be true, which I do not accept, it would be of quite secondary importance, and I should be obliged to press the question, but we will approach it by another route. You are an experienced businessman?"

"Yes. I suppose I am."

"Both Roger and Cyril Truscott were inexperienced boys?"

"Roger thought he knew too much for anyone to teach him anything."

"Or perhaps he was not entirely assured of the good faith of those who sought to advise him?"

"I cannot tell what he thought. He refused to take the advice of the auditors, or your own firm."

"Well, our advice may have been bad. You were acting as a trustee for both boys until Roger came of age?"

"Yes. And I'd done my duty in that for seventeen years, as no one knows better than your own firm."

Mr. Wedland-Wedland, having a long experience in the demeanour of witnesses, was aware that these questions were of an unwelcome nature, and that Mr. Rowton was restraining his irritation with an increasing difficulty. But he had felt that he might do more harm than good by an abortive protest. Now he rose.

"I am most reluctant to interpose, but are we not wandering rather far? The propriety of Mr. Rowton's actions as trustees during the last seventeen years has not been called in question in any way, and I am sure my friend does not intend to do so, or to set up that his conduct in that capacity has occasioned the murder which is now under investigation."

"So far," Leslie replied with a smile, "no one has raised the question except Mr. Rowton himself."

"That," Mr. Buxted agreed, smiling in his turn at the prosecuting counsel, "is how I understood it to be."

"That," Mr. Wedland-Wedland allowed, "may be the case; but the propriety of this cross-examination, the point of which is not easy to follow."

"I hope," Leslie said cheerfully, "to make it quite clear before I conclude."

"I am sure, Mr. Tonks," Mr. Buxted said seriously, "that you will not overstep the legitimate bounds of cross-examination. I am most reluctant to make any ruling which might embarrass the defence in such a case as this. But I must rely upon your discretion, that you will not give me cause to regret the latitude which I allow."

"If…"—Mr. Wedland-Wedland persisted, having now had an opportunity for further reflection, which he appeared to have utilised to some logical consequence—"…if I correctly understood a remark which my friend made only a few minutes ago, his defence is not that there are any extenuating circumstances, such as I need not enumerate, but that the accused is absolutely innocent of any part in, or even knowledge of the crime. If that be so, it is particularly difficult to understand the relevance of the questions which he has just put."

"The learned counsel has understood the contention of the defence quite accurately," Leslie replied. "It is that my client had no part whatever in what he regards as a most brutal and cowardly murder. So far as this case has proceeded, the present witness is the only one whose evidence connects him with it in any way. I propose to show—even if I do not go further—that Mr. Rowton's evidence is gravely inaccurate. I propose to show, on other grounds, that he is not an impartial, but a hostile witness. I propose, at the present moment, to ask him no more than two or three further questions, if it be understood that I may request that he be recalled to the box at a later stage."

Mr. Buxted said: "Very well, Mr. Tonks, pray go on."

"Now, Mr. Rowton, if you feel unwilling to state, from whatever cause, the grounds for any dispute which there may have arisen between Roger and Cyril Truscott, I am going to suggest to you what it was.

"I suggest that you advised Roger, on his coming of age, to consent to the sale of the whole of his interest in the business, and that of his brother also, at a price which he declined to accept without personal investigation.

"I suggest that, for the fortnight prior to the murder of Cyril Truscott, he was engaged in such investigation, resisting both his brother's importunity and the pressure which you were putting upon him, and at the end of that period, he rightly declined to sell."

"I did not put any pressure upon him. I gave him sound business advice."

"You still say the advice was good?"

"Yes. I do. Otherwise I should not have given it."

"Have you seen this paragraph?" He passed up the newspaper which lay before him.

Mr. Rowton read it, and the paper was passed to Mr. Buxted, at his request, and then to Mr. Wedland-Wedland.

"And, having read that, do you still say that your advice was sound?"

"It was sound advice on the knowledge that I then had."

"You had no knowledge that this huge contract might be secured? Did you mention the possibility to these boys when you advised them to sell their shares?"

"They were not to be sold to me."

"That was not what I asked you."

"I did not expect that our estimate would be accepted. Even now, it is no more than a newspaper report."

"So you did not mention it?"

"I may not have done so. The advice I gave was on more general grounds."

Leslie turned to the magistrate to say: "I do not propose to ask further questions now, if it be understood that this witness may be recalled when other evidence has been taken."

He felt that, if he should go further before he knew the time at which the telephone message had been received, he might be digging a pit for his own feet.

Mr. Buxted said: "Very well, Mr. Tonks."

"In that case," Mr. Wedland-Wedland said, "I will reserve my re-examination also."

Mr. Rowton stepped down, and the name of Albert Menzies having been called, that gentleman entered the court, and made his way to the witness box.

CHAPTER XVII.

ALBERT MENZIES proved to be a good witness from the lawyers' standpoint. He was unhurried and self-possessed. He gave his answers clearly, and did not go beyond the scope of the question.

He stated that at 1:00 P.M. on Wednesday, the 12th instant, when the remainder of the office staff of Truscott & Rowton had been leaving for lunch, he had gone to Mr. Rowton's office, with a report which he had been instructed to take to him.

"Did you go into his office?"

"No. He was coming out. I met him at the door."

"What happened then?"

"He told me to put it on his desk, and he would go into it after lunch."

"Did you do so?"

"No. He kept it in his hand, and asked me some questions about it."

"Still standing at the door of his office?"

"Yes."

"At what time would this be?"

"About five past one."

"And what happened then?"

"The door of Mr. Roger Truscott's room opened. There was some altercation there between Mr. Roger and Mr. Cyril."

"Did you hear what was said?"

"Not very clearly. I was attending to what Mr. Rowton was saying to me."

"But you noticed that there was—in your own word—an altercation?"

"Yes. I think Mr. Roger wanted to leave, and Mr. Cyril stood in his way."

"How did it end?"

"Mr. Cyril walked to the door of the private stairs, shouting something about coming back to get what he wanted, and Mr. Roger followed him."

"Followed him out?"

"Yes. They both went through the door."

"And then?"

"Then there was a shot."

"How soon after?"

"Almost at once."

"A minute?"

"Oh, less than that."

"Less than a minute. And what happened then?"

"Mr. Rowton said: 'What's that, Menzies?' and I ran to the door."

"What did you see?"

"I saw Mr. Roger go out by the door at the foot of the stairs."

"You are quite sure of that?"

"Yes."

"Did he close the door after him?"

"Yes."

"Did you see anything else?"

"I saw what looked like a man's body at the foot of the stairs, and I think I called out. Mr. Rowton came, and then Bellman, and we went down together. We found Mr. Cyril lying dead."

"Anything else?"

"There was a gun lying on the stairs near the top."

"What did you do then?"

"Mr. Rowton told us not to touch anything. He told me to phone Scotland Yard."

"And you did that?"

"Yes."

"You are quite certain that it was Roger Truscott whom you saw go out at the street door?"

"Yes."

"There was no one else on the stairs?"

"No."

"Quite certain?"

"Quite."

"Very well, that will do."

Mr. Wedland-Wedland sat down, and Mr. Tonks rose.

"You have said that Mr. Roger was behind Mr. Cyril when they went out?"

"Yes."

"You are certain of that?"

"Yes."

"So that if your memory were wrong on that point, it might be wrong on others equally important?"

"It isn't wrong about that."

"Well, we shall see. You're sure you touched nothing before you called the police?"

"No."

"You just went down together, and Mr. Rowton told you at once to phone up the police?"

"Yes."

"And, of course, you went straightway and did what you were told?"

"Yes."

"Very well. Now, about the man who you say went out at the door at the foot of the stairs. What makes you so sure it was Roger Truscott? The stairs are rather dark, are they not?"

"Not when the street door opens."

"The street door was already open when you looked down?"

There was a moment's perhaps natural hesitation before the reply came: "Yes, it was."

"Then you would only have seen the back of anyone going out? And a very momentary glimpse?"

"It wasn't long."

"I should think not. How many times had you seen Mr. Roger Truscott before?"

"He'd been round the offices for about a fortnight."

"But not seeing much of you?"

"Yes. On and off. He was asking me about different things."

"Anyway, you only caught a momentary glimpse of a man's back, two flights below?"

"I saw him clearly enough."

"You say that, when the sound of the shot was heard, Mr. Rowton told you to go at once to see what it was. Did you do that?"

"Yes."

"And how far is the door of Mr. Rowton's room, outside which you were standing, from the one at the head of the stairs?"

"About eight or ten yards."

"Or less?"

"Possibly a little less."

"Should you like to run down two flights of stairs while someone else was walking eight yards?"

"No. I am not a very active man."

"Do you think anyone would?"

"I haven't considered it."

"Well, consider it now."

"He must have been very quick."

"In other words, it couldn't be done?"

"I can't agree about that, because I know that it was."

Mr. Tonks sat down, and Mr. Wedland-Wedland re-examined his witness.

"However long or short your view may have been, you are quite certain, and do, in fact, swear that it was Roger Truscott, the man you now see in the dock, who went out of that door?"

"Yes."

"And you are certain that there was no one else on the stairs at the time?"

"Yes. We went down them at once."

"So that no one could have been nearer than Roger Truscott, or even as near?"

"No. They couldn't."

"And when you walked across to open the door at the head of the stairs, you were not moving with the speed of one who escapes from a place where he has just shot his brother?"

"No."

The witness left the box, and Mr. Buxted spoke: "Mr. Wedland-Wedland, I think we should have a plan of these premises. You can have it here by the morning? Very good. Thank you. I think this may be a convenient point at which to adjourn."

But Inspector Byfleet was leaning over from the gangway to speak to the prosecuting counsel, who rose to say: "If you please, there is the police witness here for whom you asked. I understand that his evidence will not take more than three minutes."

Mr. Buxted agreed to hear him, and Sergeant Horton, being sworn, stated that he had taken the call from the offices of Truscott & Rowton on the 12th inst. He produced the call-book. The time entered was 1:18 P.M.

"That," Mr. Wedland-Wedland remarked, "is no evidence of the time at which Menzies first attempted to get through."

Mr. Tonks rose to ask: "Police calls have preferential rights on the exchange? They are put through immediately?"

The witness agreed.

CHAPTER XVIII.

MR. TONKS considered his (or rather his clients') position, and was anxious. He considered himself as an advocate and was not pleased. He had had a long conference with Roger, which was to be renewed in the morning. He had the consolation of knowing that Roger appreciated his efforts, to which Mr. Weatherhead had also given some praise.

"This question of time," he had said, "is a fine point, but you have driven it in, and it may prove to be the thin end of a wedge, which will split open a rotten core. That is, if Rowton and Menzies are telling less than the truth, as I think they are. There is the porter's evidence still to come."

"Yes," Leslie had replied, "and they will have till the morning to trim his tale."

"That's a pity which can't be helped, but I don't think Inspector Byfleet, or Wedland-Wedland either, is a man who would press a charge in which he didn't believe."

Leslie had to take what consolation he could from that. He knew that Bellman would have made a statement already, the substance of which would be set out in the brief. It would be awkward to make a change now to account for five minutes—at least five—which seemed to have disappeared.

To that extent—it might be said to that vital extent—the event had justified his own courage, and Roger's protest of ignorance. For there had been the evident risk that, in pressing for the exact time at which the call was received, and in emphasising its importance, he might have established the case for the prosecution to an impregnable strength. Suppose the time should have been recorded at 1:08 instead of 1:18 P.M.?

He had the satisfaction, also, of knowing that he was considered by his brother lawyers, who had crowded the benches reserved to the profession, as having the best of the day. But he knew that he must not allow too much meaning to that. His defence, by its unexpected boldness, had driven in the outposts of an enemy which had been sure (yet perhaps not oversure?) of its own strength. But what use was there in that, if he should be faced with interior walls which he could not storm?"

Those who had listened and watched had been led to expect that he would have some dramatic surprise with which to confound the prosecution, when the time should come for him to open Roger's defence. He had hinted at another witness, and had seen Inspector Byfleet's sudden glance of puzzled surprise. Would the new witness be an anticlimax to the expectation his words had raised?

When he summarised the events of the day, he saw two points for satisfaction.

First, there had been the news of the placing of the Brazilian contract (which had been confirmed in later editions). And that suggested that Roger's instinctive judgement had been right, and, with approximately equal certainty, that Rowton's persuasion to sell had been biased—presumably by self-interest—at least to the verge of fraud. If he could only show that Rowton had known at an earlier date that that contract would be secured!

Yet he must not forget that it was not Rowton who was on trial, nor was the issue of a financial character. Had it been Roger who had been murdered—but Cyril had been active and vehement for the sale of the shares. Say that Rowton's advice were honest or insincere, it made no difference to the fact that Cyril was on his side, and he was almost the last man in the world whom, at that moment, he should have been anxious to kill.

Yet the second point which he had gained—that fourteen minutes (as he calculated) which had elapsed between Roger leaving the building, and the calling of the police—remained—and it was too long. It suggested conferences over the dead body—possibly the discussion of a common tale—before the police were called.

He must make the utmost of that. How much it would be must be hard to guess until Bellman had told his tale. If the brother who had been making the trouble had been shot—but that Mr. Rowton should deliberately murder Cyril (or encourage Menzies to do it?) was absurd. Beside that, they were not the type of men who were likely to be guilty of homicidal crime.

So he reviewed the position, with an aching head which made optimism more than usually difficult. When he thought of his own conduct of the proceedings, he was still unsatisfied. He was doubtful of the wisdom of so many things he had said: could think of so many questions he might have asked. Perhaps he should not have trusted his own ability, but have briefed a counsel of practised skill in handling criminal cases of such gravity, and so relieved himself of a responsibility which was not easy to bear.

Meanwhile, Roger lay through a wakeful night with emotions too confused for any settled mood of pain or pleasure, of hope or apprehension, to gain control.

He did not spare Leslie Tonks' lack of satisfaction with his own efforts. He felt a debt of gratitude to a lawyer who had believed what must have sounded most improbable protests of innocence, and had had the courage to challenge evidence which had seemed—which might still prove to be—too strong to be overset. And, as he had listened, he had recognised the subtle change of atmosphere which had followed from the spirit in which his innocence had been asserted, and the prosecution's witnesses challenged. His lawyer had not taken the tone of one who is there to say what can yet be said for a guilty man.

And he saw also that the fact of that interval of nearly fifteen minutes between his leaving and the call to the police might yet prove sufficient to open the sinister gates which had closed upon him. The magistrate's request for a plan of the office floor had been a recognition that there was something that must be probed beneath the surface assertions which had seemed to condemn him beyond defence. The wall of lies were still there in unbroken strength, but the tide of truth was sapping around its walls.

He had more decided, if less vital, reason for satisfaction in the news that the Brazilian contract, of which he had known nothing until that day, had been secured by the firm. He did not judge Rowton with having been aware of that probability at an earlier date. He still knew nothing which would justify such a suspicion. But suppose he had known the amount of the rival estimate when their own had been sent in? Suppose Rowton had been squared in some way to send in a higher estimate, so that Lessings' would get the contract, as the market had evidently anticipated that they would do? Suppose that it had not been foreseen that the Brazilian Government might prefer the higher figure in view of the reputation of the older firm?

He had already learnt enough of the position to know what Rowton's reply would be. He would say that they were unable to quote as low as Lessings, being inferior in up-to-date machinery and other facilities for working at cut prices, which only fresh capital could provide. It had been one of his foremost arguments at that first lunch, when he had undertaken to explain the reasons for which he advised the sale. He would say that this acceptance of the higher estimate was a piece of unexpected good fortune, on which no sound businessman would gamble before it came. It would be plausible and it might even be true.

Yet the incident increased Roger's instinctive feeling that he had been surrounded by a treachery that he could not prove. And, in any event, the news had been doubly good. It meant that he could probably value his own and his brother's shares at twice the figure of yesterday, perhaps at much more than that. And it made it impossible for anyone to say that Cyril's quarrel with him had its cause in a foolish obstinacy in which he would have sacrificed his brother's interests as well as his own. He had the satisfaction of one who has been justified by the event.

But when he thought of "his brother's shares," the question came for the first time to his mind: whose shares were they today? He supposed that they must be his, and was led to wonder whether he would have to face the dreadful suggestion that he had shot Cyril so that the whole inheritance might be his. Even the knowledge of a fortune that has been made secure and doubled in a day is no sufficient satisfaction to one who lies in a prison cell on a charge of having taken his brother's life. And then his thoughts wandered again.

She had been in one of the seats at the side, where he could see her face from the dock if he looked her way—or she him. But he could watch her, if he would, without much probability that his own eyes would be met, for she was not there to look idly round, as were the spectators who had fought their way to the few available seats in that crowded court. She was there (he guessed correctly by Mr. Boddington's instructions, though he was puzzled as to why he should be sufficiently interested to spare her for such a purpose) to take down the evidence.

And he saw that she was doing it in no perfunctory spirit. There could have been few words spoken in court that day that her quick pencil did not record. Even when the official reporters paused at interchanges which they did not think it necessary to set down, her pencil was active still.

But even in the absorbing interest of that drama, at which the process of English law made him no more than a spectator, who could doze if he would (as some criminals will) while the quiet deadly contest of lawyers' wits fought out an issue which had his honour, perhaps his life, as the stake that the winners drew—even then, his eyes had turned at times to watch her in half-oblivion of the evidence that was incredibly fastening upon him the crime of his brother's death. He knew her only as one who had repulsed his diffident, clumsy advances, whose face had haunted his dreams in that time that seemed as remotely past, and was no more than ten days away. And then, in the pause when Ellis Rowton had left the box, and the name of Albert Menzies was being called, and there had been the rustle and whispering which such moments allow, she had looked up, and their eyes had met.

She had looked at him in a questioning, puzzled doubt, as though she saw that there was enigma, but could not guess what its answer might prove to be; and he had looked back, until in a sudden way, her glance changed, and he had become aware that he looked into the eyes of a friend—of one who believed him guiltless, with a belief which became a quick trouble to her, but had been sufficient to make him glad. It had raised his mood, and been half the cause that he had been able to speak to Leslie Tonks at a later hour in a hopeful, almost confident way.

Could he lose, with so much that the world held which the young can take? He had a stubborn rather than a sanguine spirit, one that always saw defeat as a likely thing, but would go on fighting no less, and no worse, for the clear vision he had. He did not think that it would be easy to break the net that was round him now. And yet— that he could be convicted of a crime in which he had not had the remotest part, of which he knew nothing, of the truth of which he could make no guess—it seemed too dreadful a possibility to admit to his mind. And to be convicted meant to be hanged. There could be no doubt about that. To shoot a brother in the back is not a deed for which much sympathy can be felt, and if the defence can offer no palliating circumstance—nothing but stubborn, useless denial— there can be no doubt what the end will be.

But it was a nightmare too dreadful for waking truth. He remembered once, at a college dinner at which a famous lawyer had been a guest, that he had heard him say that innocent men are not convicted in English courts. He had said it confidently, as one stating a fact which could only be challenged by very prejudiced men.

But there was no consolation in that memory, for it went on to a question that a college professor asked: "What about Crippen?" And the lawyer had paused, and said, "Well, at worst, you can say that that was a good guess."

He had gone on to say that if Crippen were innocent, he had hanged himself. "If his wife poisoned herself, or he tried to drug her and overdid it, he should have told the truth, but the defence he put up was bound to fail."

And if he were hanged, would not men say the same thing about him? "There was something about that Truscott case"—so he imagined the words—"that didn't ever come out. There must have been more motive, or more provocation, or more—something—than will ever be known; but Roger Truscott's defence gave him no chance. What was the sense in saying he wasn't there, when everyone knew he was?"

The tale that he had heard from two mouths in the witness box was untrue. There could be no doubt of that; for he knew that, when he went down the stairs, he had left his brother behind.

When Ellis Rowton and Menzies swore that Cyril had gone out first they were wrong, but it was not beyond possibility that they believed what they said: that memory had failed, as it often will. But when they spoke of the shot that came so instantly after he went through the door—when Menzies spoke of having seen him go out to the street—it was hard to think that less than deliberate perjury could explain the tale.

Yet—with what object? And what had happened which had made that perjury necessary, or, at least, given them opportunity to use it against him? That was the real question. It was a sphinx-like riddle by which he might save his life, if he could guess the answer correctly. With such a stake, surely he could not fail!

He went on to imagine many wild or improbable, many possible and some impossible things—needless to be recited here, for they were all wrong. But in such speculations he fell asleep, and did not wake till he was roused by the routine of life in the prison cells.

CHAPTER XIX.

MR. WEATHERHEAD walked with his partner to the court. He was not usually optimistic. He had the cautions of temperament and of years, added to that which becomes habitual to those who practise amid the deadly quicksands of law. But he was inclined to be encouraging now.

"I think," he said, "you've found their weak spot, and it's something more than a thin link in a chain of proof, good enough to bamboozle a jury, or use to urge a reprieve. There was something going on in that quarter of an hour, more than Rowton admits, and the fact that Menzies tells the same tale only means that it's a deliberate concealment, on which they've agreed from the first. I don't need to point out all the implications of that."

"No. But have you any theory of what did happen? That's where I'm pulled up."

"I can't say I have. Not any guess that seems sufficiently probable to divide it from its wilder companions. But, I think, when you've examined Bellman, we both may."

"I wish I could have had him in the box yesterday, before they had a chance to talk to him, and a night to think out what it will be best for him to say."

"But I'm not sure that you're right, even about that. If they'd got a prepared tale, he'd just have gone confidently into the box, and said what Menzies had said before. He wouldn't have known that the tale was being seriously attacked. Now he'll have read the newspaper reports, whatever else may or may not have been said to him, and he'll have had a night in which to have lost his nerve. If you go at him boldly, you may find he'll break down, and you'll have a walkover."

It was an alluring prospect, and Leslie wished it could be something more than a pleasant dream. He knew that if he could bring the prosecution to such an end, he would have made a reputation that half a century might not dim, with the satisfactory detail of saving his client's life to be added thereto.

"I'll go at him boldly enough," he said, "if that's what you advise. But I doubt, from what Evans reports, that he'll break down of himself."

"Evans didn't get much?"

"He got nothing, beyond the information that the man won't talk. He refused to discuss the murder even with other employees, or with some cronies he meets at night in the Wheatsheaf bar. Evans decided, from what he heard, that it would be useless to approach him directly, and might do harm. All he found out that's any use to us is that his army record was good, and he's been at Truscott & Rowton's for the last eight years."

"If he is a man of good character."

"You mean he's all the more important? So he is—either way. It's not necessarily good news for us. It all depends upon what he says. But I don't think he'll be an easy witness to rattle. Evans' report was: 'You'll find he's a man who doesn't slobber his words.' But he's got that extra five minutes to explain, all the same, and he's got to do it with something better than a shut mouth."

"Yet that's what you've got most to dread. If he says he didn't notice the time particularly, and only knows that Menzies telephoned when he was told, you can't carry it much further with him. He's more likely to fall over if they've tried to cook up something during the night to explain the time. But I've noticed one thing often enough, a man can sometimes tell a lie that you can't upset, even though you feel certain it isn't true; but if two men try it on, it's not twice as hard, it's more like fifty times as hard for them to keep it up with a firm front, and when you come to three taking a hand...."

"Yes. But, if they can keep it up?"

Mr. Weatherhead could not deny that, but the need for answer did not arise. They had already reached the solicitors' room as this conversation proceeded, and now they went into court together.

As soon as Mr. Buxted was seated, Mr. Wedland-Wedland rose to put in the plan of the premises for which the magistrate had asked on the previous afternoon. It showed Mr. Rowton's office, with the adjacent room which had been allotted to Roger Truscott, and the main office beyond. The full breadth of the main office was twenty-nine feet, but that of Mr. Rowton's room was sixteen feet, so that the space which must be crossed to the door of the private stairs would have been little more than three yards, but the two doors were not opposite to one another, the actual distance being between six and seven yards.

Mr. Buxted studied it carefully, but made no comment. He said: "You will like to see this, Mr. Tonks."

The plan was passed down to Leslie, but it could tell him little he did not already know, for he had been in Mr. Rowton's office on several occasions. It was the distance between the two doors in which he was interested, and that proved to be even less than had been suggested on the previous day.

Mr. Buxted was anxious to get ahead. "You have another witness, Mr. Wedland-Wedland?" Alfred Bellman entered the box.

Leslie looked at a short, stocky man with a close-cut crop of greying hair, and light-blue, rather bloodshot eyes in a brick-red face, who stood with military stiffness in the witness box, and took the oath in a routine, unemotional way.

Mr. Wedland-Wedland elicited with sufficient brevity that he had been in the army before the war. Northumberland Fusiliers. Afterwards, M.G.C. Twice wounded. France and Salonika. Last year of war was at Aldershot, training recruits. Discharged with pension of sergeant-major in 1924. Three medals.

"Now, Mr. Bellman, we come to your present occupation. For the last eight years you have been continuously in the employment of Truscott & Rowton Ltd?"

"Yes, sir, eight years last March."

"And is it one of your duties there to clear up the offices when the staff goes to lunch at midday?"

"Yes, sir."

"Were you engaged in this way on Wednesday, the 12th inst., shortly after 1:00 P.M.?"

"Yes, sir, I was sprinkling the floor."

"You would be doing that immediately the clerks went out, preparatory to sweeping it?"

"Yes, sir, I always sprinkled it first."

"And you were interrupted in this work? Perhaps you had better tell the court what you saw in your own way.

"I can't say I saw much, sir. I was attending to my own work."

Leslie looked keenly at the man with a sudden hope. Was he going to refuse to confirm, if not to deny, enough to give him a chance against the two earlier witnesses? He looked at the prosecuting counsel, but, if that gentleman were disconcerted by the reply, he was too adroit to let it appear.

He said, as one who humours an awkward child: "Very well. If you didn't see much, tell the court what you heard."

"I heard a shot on the stairs."

"You knew what it was?"

"Yes, sir, I'd heard a few before then."

"I've no doubt you had. And what happened after that?"

"Mr. Menzies went to the door of the stairs, and called out. Then Mr. Rowton went, and I followed. We went down, and there was a man dead at the bottom."

"Mr. Cyril Truscott?"

"Yes, sir. That's who they said it was. I hadn't known him before. Not to notice, that is."

"He was dead when you first went down?"

"You might call it that. He was done for, sure enough. You could tell that by how he lay."

"And what happened then?"

"Mr. Rowton said we'd best touch nothing till the police came."

"How long was that?"

"It might have been twenty minutes, or a bit less."

"Now we'll go back to the time before you heard the shot. Had you seen anyone go out through the door before that?"

"Yes, sir. Just before."

"Did you see who it was?"

"Not to notice particular."

"Was it Mr. Cyril Truscott? The man you found dead at the foot of the stairs?"

"No, it wasn't him."

"What makes you sure of that?"

"He hadn't got on a dark suit."

"Who hadn't?"

"The man I saw crossing the floor."

"And the dead man had?"

"Yes, sir."

"What sort of a suit was the man wearing that you saw going out?"

"It was something light."

"Look at the prisoner. Was it that kind of suit?"

"About that."

"Wait a moment," Mr. Buxted interposed. "I want to be quite clear about this." He turned to the witness. "What I understand you to say is that a man in a light suit crossed from the private offices to the door at the head of the stairs, and went out immediately before you heard the shot. This man was wearing a light suit, but beyond that, you could not identify him?"

"Yes, sir, that's got it right."

"Now look carefully at the prisoner. Do you swear that you cannot say that he was the man?"

"No, sir. I didn't notice, not that particular."

"Could you swear that the prisoner is not the man?"

"No, sir, I couldn't say either way."

"Very well. Go on, Mr. Wedland-Wedland."

But that gentleman said that he had no further questions to ask. Mr. Tonks rose.

"You have said that you cannot identify the man who went out immediately before the shot was fired. Did you notice anyone go out before him?"

"No, I can't say I did."

"Can you say that there was no one else—only the one?"

"No, I can't say either way. I was just coming along, watering the floor."

Leslie sat down, and Mr. Wedland-Wedland said that that was his case.

Mr. Buxted said: "Now, Mr. Tonks." And observed as he said it that that gentleman was talking earnestly to Mr. Weatherhead.

The court waited in some curiosity of expectation as this whispered conversation proceeded, and was followed by a similar and somewhat longer colloquy between Mr. Tonks and the prisoner.

The fact was that, as Mr. Weatherhead had heard Bellman's evidence, he had changed his mind radically. He saw (and knew that Leslie must be realising also) that they had drawn an unexpected blank. Bellman, repeating the tale that they had heard twice already and stoutly asserting that every word was true, would have been an anticipated obstacle, and Leslie had prepared several neat and ingenious snares to confuse and trap him, if he had come with a lying tale. But that he should have been left at the foot of the stair, natural as it was, had not crossed his mind. Obviously, it would be waste of words to ask him at what time Menzies had telephoned, or what had prevented him from doing it five or ten minutes earlier than he had. If his story were true, he knew nothing about it. And as to what had happened earlier, his profession of very limited observation was more difficult to discredit, and might be an even more deadly weapon in the hands of the prosecution, than a more complete and literal support of the evidence of the previous witnesses.

"Might it not," he whispered, "be better to reserve the defence?"

He spoke to one who was as conscious as himself of an unexpected obstruction, of a position which needed time for consideration. To say that the accused reserved his defence was to make committal certain, but was it not certain in either event? There would be at least three weeks for further enquiry and consideration before the trial could come on. There would be the opportunity to brief counsel more experienced in a criminal trial of this complexion and gravity. To go on now might be to jeopardise a more skilful defence at a later stage.

Leslie saw this, and the arguments of caution and cowardice were not easy to separate in his mind. But he saw also that to surrender now, though it might be in no worse guise than that of a strategic retreat, would be so inconsistent with the tone he had taken on the previous day, as to make it seem no more than the foolish demonstration of an inexperienced advocate. Better than what he had done—far better—would it have been to have accepted all that was said without comment and spring the full strength of the defence, be it much or little, as a surprise when the trial came. Had he not actually said that he would ask the magistrate to dismiss the charge? He could imagine how caustic would be the comments of Purvis-Jones, or any other of the leading criminal advocates, if he should be briefed for the defence of a case which had been so mishandled in the magistrate's court. But all this was beside the mark. His client's interests were the sole consideration which he should admit to his mind.

And his client must be consulted before he could change a decision which had been made that morning, and which had become the instructions on which he was bound to act.

So the whispered discussion with his partner was followed by a whispered discussion with the prisoner, as Leslie leaned over the edge of the dock, and the two policemen who sat on either side assumed the unhearing aspect of men more wooden than even a policeman can ever be.

And Roger, as aware as his legal advisers that the third witness had foiled their hopes, and with greater cause for depression than they, having so much greater a stake, had a moment's weakness, in which he was tempted to delay what looked as yet to be no more than a hopeless effort; but the stubbornness which was at the core of his nature, which had enabled him to resist every argument and cajolery concentrated upon him to induce him to sell the shares, and which his quiet unassertive manner would often belie, gave a better answer, even before he caught Diana Morton's eyes fixed upon him (her pencil idle now, in the pause which this consultation gave) with an anxious, expectant look, as though she guessed and feared, and yet refused to believe what the cause of hesitation might be.

"You know what I think," he said. "I think the case is no more than some clever lies, though I can't guess what happened, or why they are trying to fasten it on me in the way they do. I don't want to go against your advice—it isn't likely I should—but I think when anyone has an accusation like this made against him, he ought to deny it, the first chance he gets."

Leslie said: "Then we go on as arranged." He turned to address the court.

"I might ask you at once," he said, "to dismiss the charge on the ground that the evidence for the prosecution is so deficient in probability, and of such a character, that no jury would convict upon i"

"I am afraid," Mr. Buxted interrupted, in his most magisterial tone, "I cannot follow you there. As the evidence now stands, there is certainly a case to answer."

"I propose to submit in due course that it is evidence which will not endure analysis," Leslie replied, with more confidence of demeanour than his inward conviction warranted, "but my client is anxious for an opportunity of denying on oath the charge which has been made against him. I call Roger Truscott."

With a policeman at his elbow, as though he were a dangerous animal who must not be let loose in that crowded court, Roger left the dock for the witness box.

CHAPTER XX.

To many inexperienced and sensitive people, it would be regarded as an unpleasant ordeal to give evidence in the witness box of a criminal court, even though they might themselves be free from direct responsibility concerning the case which had brought them there; and it is one that may be sufficient to shake the nerve of all but the most courageous, if it be done with the consciousness that liberty or life itself may be staked upon the accuracy and wisdom of the replies which can be promptly given to questions which may be cunningly devised to confuse and then confound them, that even a fault of demeanour may be sufficient to tilt a trembling scale.

But Roger found at first, as many another witness had done before him, that the ordeal was much less than it had appeared to his own fears.

Guided by the skilful questions, soothed by the friendly tone of his own lawyer, he told the tale of his relations with his brother, of his coming to London, of the events that followed, including those of the fatal morning, with a quiet sincerity of manner which won a momentary belief from all who heard, excepting those with sufficient experience of criminal courts to know how often the story that sounds convincing as the witness is shepherded through it by his own advocate, will be transformed into the improbable or grotesque when subjected to a few further queries from a different angle.

For half an hour he told his story with a growing confidence, until the final questions came:

"And you are sure that, when you went out, you left your brother behind?"

"Yes, I am quite positive."

"And you had no part in his murder whatever, nor even knowledge that it had occurred?"

"I knew nothing of it until Inspector Byfleet arrested me. I could scarcely believe it then."

"And you have no idea of whom the murderer may be?"

"No, I wish I had."

And then Mr. Wedland-Wedland had risen, and he was being addressed in a different tone.

"Now, Mr. Truscott, you have told us something about the quarrel between your brother and yourself, and you say that it was all on his side. You had no occasion to feel angry with him? Let me ask you a question to which you should listen carefully. *Would it be too much to say that for him to have lived would have been fatal to all your plans?*"

Mr. Wedland-Wedland asked this question with his eyes fixed on the witness as though to fascinate him to the confession of his natural baseness. The words were slow, insistent, menacing. They were followed by a tense silence in the listening court, which observed that the demeanour of the witness was quickly changed from its former confidence. He looked confused, and his face flushed with emotions which the spectators could only guess.

"I don't know," he said, "in the least, what you mean."

"Oh, yes, you do. Think again and then answer the question."

"I hadn't any plans that were hostile to Cyril. I wanted to do the best I could for both of us."

"That is no answer."

"I think it is. I don't really know what the question means."

"No? Then I will give you a little help. For the moment, I am going to accept your version of this quarrel. We do not know how different it might sound if the dead boy were here to give us his own account. You say that you were determined that the firm should be carried on in your own way against the advice of all the officers of the company, of its financial and legal advisers, and in spite of the protests of your brother, whose interests were as much involved as your own. Is that right or wrong?"

"I should put it rather differently."

"I daresay you would. What I asked you was, is it right or wrong?"

"It is substantially right."

"Substantially right. And you have told us that your brother was opposed—violently opposed—to this policy. He wanted to realise the shares and have money to spend?"

"Yes."

"Do you suppose that he would have changed his attitude in eighteen months?"

"I couldn't possibly answer that."

"But there is at least a great probability that he would still have wanted to sell?"

"It is quite possible."

"I suggest to you that it is much more than possible. That by your own description of his disposition, he would have wished to realise his fortune, even if your own sanguine anticipations of the result of your inexperienced control of the business had been fulfilled—that he would have thought it best to take the cash 'while the going's good,' as he might have put it? Where would you have been then? Could you have bought the shares?"

"No. I don't see how I could. I have never considered such a contingency."

"No? Do you really ask the court to believe that? Have you not told us that your mind was fixed on continuing this business as you believed that your father would have wished you to do? Do you ask the court to believe that you never considered what the position would be in eighteen months from now, when your brother's shares must pass out of your own control?"

"I was anxious that the value of his shares should not be decreased by that time."

"Doubtless you were. But again that is not what I asked. We know the position from your own lips. You had rejected the plan of amalgamation which Mr. Rowton, with his prolonged experience of the business, had urged upon you. You had refused to listen to your brother's pleading that you should take the same course. On that Wednesday morning you had learnt finally—you say violently—from your brother's lips that he would neither accept your advice, nor relax his efforts to induce you to sell his shares. If you stood out—as you have told us that you were resolved to do with an obstinacy which continued even when this charge was overhanging your head—what would your position be in eighteen months, when you would control no more than sixty thousand of the hundred and fifty thousand shares which are the total capital of the firm, when your brother's voting power would be as much as your own, and would be almost certainly thrown into the scale against you in support of those who would be able, with his help, to take the control out of your hands?"

"If Cyril had continued to wish to sell his shares, he could have done so then. I saw that, of course, but I can't say I had thought much about its consequences. I had enough to worry about in deciding what to do at this time. It's a monstrous thing to suggest that I should have thought of killing Cyril for such a cause."

The witness's voice rose to a tone of vibrant indignation as he made this protest, that many of those who heard were disposed to respond with a kindred feeling of instinctive rather than reasoned sympathy and belief; but Mr. Wedland-Wedland had a long experience in countering such emotional outbursts, whether real or simulated.

Was he not himself expert in playing upon a jury's emotions, with no reality of passion, and often no reality of conviction behind his words?

"Yes," he said, "we will agree that fratricide is always a monstrous crime. Yet within an hour of your realisation that your brother would never come to your way of thinking about those shares, he lay dead on the office stairs which none had descended but you and he. I put it to you again that, on that morning, if not before, you saw that there was only one way by which you could hope to achieve the ambition which filled your thoughts—*and that way was your brother's death.*"

"And I say that it is a monstrous thought that never entered my mind."

"You do not deny that you did stand to benefit by his death?"

"No, I don't deny that. I suppose when anyone dies, someone else usually does benefit, but it doesn't follow that they killed them to get it."

"No—but they don't all die in the same way. Can you suggest the name of anyone but yourself who would benefit by his death?"

"No."

"Or anyone who had a quarrel with him?"

"No, I wish I could."

"Probably you do. He had no quarrel with Mr. Rowton, had he?"

"No, I don't think he had."

"In fact, he was supporting Mr. Rowton's opinion against your own? We might say that it was as much to Mr. Rowton's interest that he should remain alive, as it was to yours that he should die?"

"I never wished him to die. I never had such a thought."

"You would do better to answer the question than to indulge in these hysterical outbursts. I say it was as much to Mr. Rowton's interest that he should remain alive as it was to yours that he should die. Do you deny that?"

"I don't know how it might affect Mr. Rowton's interests."

"Oh, yes, you do. You know that your brother's death would be calculated to transform Mr. Rowton's subordination to you from a temporary to a permanent position. It was about the last thing he could wish. Can you suggest any reason whatever why he, and two other independent witnesses, should give false evidence against you?"

"No, I don't understand it. I only know that it isn't true."

"But if it is true, it follows that you must have shot your brother with your own hand?"

"If it implies that, it is wrong."

"It is a case of your word alone against the fact that you were the only person living whom you can suggest as having any motive to wish for your brother's death, and the evidence of three witnesses who saw you follow him down the stairs?"

"You mean two, not three."

"We won't argue about that. You admit that two witnesses saw you follow him out?"

"Of course I don't. I've said already that I went out first."

"Do you still think it is any use to persist in a statement which is contradicted by all independent evidence, and leaves the fact that your brother was shot in the back—in the back, remember—as a mystery for which you have not any explanation, however improbable, to offer the court?"

"I can only say that I have told the truth, and I can't say what may have happened after I left."

"And that's the best you can say!"

With that exclamation, Mr. Wedland-Wedland sat down. He added, in a half-audible aside to Mr. Bayley-Atkinson, "And I should call it about the thinnest defence that I've ever heard."

Mr. Tonks rose to re-examine. He felt that, so far as Roger's denial of any knowledge of the crime was concerned, they had reached a point at which nothing more could be usefully asked. It had become a matter for argument only. But there was one further point he wished to bring out.

He asked: "Until your coming of age, at the beginning of the present month, you were in receipt of a quarterly allowance, which was, in fact, remitted to you through my own firm?"

"Yes."

"Its amount was £400?"

"Yes, £100 quarterly."

"Was it sufficient for your requirements?"

"It was more than I needed."

"Did your brother have the same amount?"

"Yes, since he came up to the University."

"Was it sufficient for him?"

"Not always."

"And you made up his deficiencies?"

"Yes, sometimes."

"To what total amount?"

119

"About five or six hundred pounds."

"You had lent him that much?"

"Not exactly lent. I mean, I never thought of his paying it back."

"Then why did you do it?"

"He always needed more money than I did."

"It was just generosity, or brotherly affection?"

"I only let him have what I didn't need."

"And when he came up to Town on the last occasion?"

"I let him have £20."

"When?"

"When I met him at the Royalty on Tuesday night."

"Why £20?"

"It was all I could spare that day."

"Had he asked you to bring him money?"

"No, but I knew he always wanted some to spend when he came up."

"Did you offer him more?"

"I said I'd seen the bank, and they were willing to grant a loan of £500 on our joint names; so that he could have that."

"When could he have it?"

"When he came to see me on Wednesday morning."

"Did he have it then?"

"No, he refused to talk about anything but the shares being sold."

"Very well, that is all."

It seemed that Roger was to leave the witness box at last, but Mr. Wedland-Wedland rose quickly for a concluding question:

"So that it was on the Wednesday morning that the final effort to obtain your brother's support for the course on which you were resolved—the offer of this £500—may be said to have definitely failed?"

"I was meaning to talk it over with him again in the afternoon."

"But you had done that in the morning, and he had refused to entertain it?"

"He didn't want to agree to anything that seemed like giving way about the shares."

"And when he refused that £500, you saw how useless it was to hope that he could be won over by any offer you could make?"

"I knew that he was very anxious that I should sell the shares."

"Very well, the position is plain enough."

Leslie was inclined to wonder whether he had been wise in asking those final questions, but it was too late for regret.

CHAPTER XXI.

MR. JAMES HIGHAM was the next witness. He was explicit in certainty that it had not been more than ten minutes after one when the prisoner had taken a seat opposite to his own at the Brading Restaurant.

He had not appeared disturbed or abnormal in any way. He did not appear to have hurried. His subsequent conversation had been that of a man whose mind was at ease. Even when Inspector Byfleet had accosted him, he had seemed unconcerned until he had learned the errand on which he came, and then his astonishment had seemed to be genuine, even approaching to incredulity.

"You say definitely," was Leslie's final question, "that his demeanour was not that of a guilty man?"

"I should say that he is entirely innocent, or he is the best actor I ever met."

Mr. Wedland-Wedland said that he had no questions to ask.

Mr. Higham's testimony was obviously disinterested, and was given in such a way that few could doubt its sincerity, or that it came from one who was used to estimating his fellowmen. Its effect upon the minds of those who heard it was as various as were the degrees of doubt concerning the prisoner's innocence that prevailed among them. To some it seemed to reduce the case for the prosecution to a monstrous improbability, to others, and they the more numerous, it was no more than an exhibition of the callousness that might be expected from one who would shoot his own brother in the back on so mean a quarrel.

It was with a sense of failure, though with determination that the game should be fought out to the last, that Leslie asked that Ellis Rowton should be recalled to the witness box.

"Mr. Rowton," he said, "you've had time to think over the evidence you gave yesterday, and you know the time now at which the telephone call you told Menzies to put through was received at Scotland Yard. It is established that Roger Truscott was seen leaving your premises at a time which was not later than 1:05 P.M. and may have been slightly earlier, and that he was in the Brading Restaurant not later than 1:10. Do you still say that the dead body of Cyril Truscott was discovered immediately after Roger left, and that Menzies made that call on your instructions without any intervening delay?"

"Yes, that's how it was."

"You can offer no explanation of the fact that the time when the call was received was actually eight minutes after Roger is known to have been sitting down in a restaurant five minutes' walk away?"

"No, I wasn't watching the clock. You don't at a time like that."

"Perhaps not, but the clock goes on just the same. You know now what the times were, and you have no explanation to offer?"

"No. Except that clocks aren't always the same. It doesn't seem so long to me either as you're trying to make it sound."

"So you have no explanation. Now just a word on another matter. You know now that your firm has secured the Brazilian contract, concerning which I questioned you last week?"

"Yes."

"Do you still swear that you had no knowledge of the destination of that contract until the day when it was publicly announced?"

"Yes. I cannot properly be said to have known it until I received official confirmation two days later."

"No expectation of it?"

"No. I thought it extremely unlikely that it would be placed with us."

"But you admit its importance? You would not have advised Roger Truscott to accept the price you did had you had reason to expect that the contract would be placed with your firm?"

"No. I might still have advised him to sell, but to stand out for a better price."

"And all this being as you say, did you impress upon him the importance of this contingency? As his responsible adviser, *did you ever mention it to him at all*?"

There was a moment's hesitation before the witness replied, but after that he answered with the same emphasis as before: "Yes, certainly."

"I put it to you that you kept him in absolute ignorance of the whole matter."

"And I reply that it is untrue."

Mr. Wedland-Wedland rose again: "Reluctant as I am to interrupt, I must submit that we are wandering rather far from the present charge."

"I don't think," Mr. Buxted replied, "that I can interfere at this point. I am anxious not to hamper the defence in any way, and I have already said that I rely upon it not to go beyond what is strictly relevant to the charge which it has to meet."

"I have only one further question to ask," Leslie replied. "Do you swear that there was no connection between the date by which my client was told that he must make his decision to sell his interest in the business—the date at which the option was said to close—and that on which it must become public knowledge that this huge contract had been secured by the firm?"

"Of course I cannot swear any such thing."

"Why not?"

"Because I cannot swear as to what was in the minds of those by whom the offer was made, nor what secret knowledge they may have had."

"I am asking you as to your own knowledge."

"Then I have replied already. The offer was not mine. I was to have sold my own shares at the same price."

"And for other considerations?"

"I was to have a seat on Lessing's board. There was no secret about that. They wouldn't have taken the shares at all without that."

"And no other undisclosed consideration of any kind?"

"No."

"You swear that?"

"Of course."

"Very well, we will leave it there for the time."

Mr. Tonks sat down.

Mr. Buxted lifted interrogative eyebrows at the prosecuting counsel, who did not rise. "Do you wish to re-examine, Mr. Wedland-Wedland?"

That gentleman shook his head. "I'm not interested," he said, "in the values of shares. I'm prosecuting a man for murdering his brother."

Mr. Buxted said: "Very well," and Mr. Rowton withdrew from the witness box.

Mr. Buxted asked: "Any more witnesses?" Mr. Tonks said no, but that he wished to address the court.

Mr. Buxted privately thought it a waste of time, for the idea of not committing the prisoner for trial had never seriously entered his head. He had delayed adjournment at the usual luncheon hour in the hope of ending the case in time for an afternoon's golf at Esher. He wondered how long Mr. Tonks would talk. Possibly hours. Long experience told him that the weaker his case may be, the longer will the average advocate take in labouring its defence. He was not convinced that there was nothing to be said here. But it could be said when there was a jury to listen. Yet he must not seem to be impatient with the defence. Mr. Tonks was responsible for its conduct, and had a right to be heard. And so, giving no sign of his thoughts, he said: "Then I think this will be a good time to adjourn for lunch."

Leslie went out, glad of the short respite, but with a feeling of defeat in his heart which was not the mood that the occasion required. He was sure that there was lying among the witnesses for the prosecution, but what was the use of that if he could not impress this conviction on other minds? If he could not even offer a plausible suggestion of what might have happened, if Roger were an innocent man? He felt that a more experienced counsel would have handled Rowton's cross-examination with more success. Had he sacrificed his client to his own vanity, to his desire to appear in a widely reported case? Well, there was the stronger reason that he should do his best now. He must remember that he would not be addressing the magistrate only, but a much larger audience, including, in all probability, some of those who would be called to sit on the jury at a later date.

He was occupied with these thoughts as he washed his hands in the lavatory adjoining the solicitors' room, and Johnny Pember came to the next basin.

Johnny was an apple-cheeked, young-looking solicitor, with twenty years of experience in the defence of the miscellaneous criminals who try their wits with indifferent success against those of the Metropolitan police. He was never eloquent, and not often serious, but he had a gift of ridicule that was widely feared. He was never lacking in retort, or in opportune jest, and had an alertness of mind that would rarely fail to marshal every ragged possibility of defence in the most hopeless of cases, so that the mere fact that he was retained would give it a face of courage. He probably turned the scale in his clients' favour in five percent of the cases he undertook, which is a high proportion—for any solicitor of average ability is usually sufficient to secure the release of an innocent man, and magistrates of ripe experience are not easily fooled, by whatever skill in a knave's defence.

He glanced sideways at his companion, and thought he looked at a worried man.

"Dirty work at the crossroads?" he asked. "So I should say there is. And you've done rather well at rubbing one or two of the raw spots, if you ask me. I should say you're getting some curses behind the scene. But I don't see how they'll help the young fellow to save his neck, unless you've a follow-up with some better cards than you've played yet."

"Yes," Leslie replied, knowing that he spoke to one who would never abuse a confidence given in that way. "If I could prove what went on in that ten minutes interval that they won't admit—"

"You mean you've no more idea than old Buxted himself? It's just a bluff that you hope will find a squealer among them? Well, it's a good try. Hope it scores. Mind if I give you a hint?"

"No, nor twenty."

"Well, find out who that young woman is who's taking notes all the time. A good-looker, but got brains, if you ask me."

"I think I know who you mean, though I've not had much leisure for looking round. She's Boddington's secretary—Bagley & Co., you know—the firm's auditors."

"Yes? There may be a pointer there. Or it may be Boddington that you ought to ask."

"What do you suppose that she'll be likely to know?"

"She knows Rowton's a liar."

"About what?"

"In particular, about that contract. I saw her look at him when he swore he hadn't known about it beforehand. Just a glance, and then her eyes went back to her book, but it told as much as though she'd talked for an hour."

"Thanks. Coming from Bagley's office—yes. It's worth following up. I wish she'd got a little private knowledge about who killed Cyril Truscott. I don't see how we're to get home on the share question alone, whatever we prove about that."

"No. I don't say you will. But if you start on a likely road, you never know where you'll finish up. I'm not sure that she's not friendly to Roger Truscott, and I suppose you've not been sitting the right way to notice that he spends half his time looking at her."

Leslie said: "Thanks for the tip," and shortened his lunch to make time to get hold of Evans on the telephone, and instruct him to find out all he could concerning Miss Morton, including her private address, and report to his office, if possible, before six that evening.

After that he went rapidly over the points which he wished to urge, to the detriment of Mr. Buxted's golfing prospects. As the case had proceeded, his belief that there was some deliberate lying, at the least to the concealment of vital facts, on the part of the witnesses for the prosecution, had strengthened to certainty; and with it that of Roger's innocence, which had at first been little more than the advocate's deliberate adoption of his client's tale, had acquired a similar certitude.

Indignation moved him, as he considered the implications of these beliefs, and he had to remind himself that he would not be addressing a jury, and that emotion would have little value in the arguments which he had to urge.

With these thoughts in his mind, he rose to address the court.

Having analysed the evidence in the detail which his submission required, he concluded: "I do not wish to be misunderstood as criticising the police, either for arresting my client, or for bringing the charge of murder against him. On the representations which were made to them, I think they took the right—indeed, the only possible—course.

"But I submit that further enquiry has failed to find any support for that evidence in the relationship of the brothers, the subsequent conduct of the prisoner, or the ownership of the weapon with which the crime was certainly committed, while that evidence itself has failed, under examination, to maintain even an appearance of plausibility.

"It has transpired that Roger Truscott had acted toward his brother with habitual and exceptional generosity. The quarrel of which we have heard so much was one that had been forced upon him; and, without going too deeply into matters which are not directly at issue, it has been shown that he was being wise, both for his brother and for himself, under circumstances of singular difficulty. In all the evidence we have heard, there has not been one word to suggest violence or instability of character, or anything but affectionate regard for his brother's interests, allied with a habitual generosity.

"The sole evidence against him is the statements made by Ellis Rowton, who is certainly of an unfriendly disposition, and Menzies, who is in his employment—that of Alfred Bellman is too vague to have any weight in the scale—and I submit that this evidence, such as it is—neither of them have had the hardihood to say that they saw the crime committed—becomes incredible when it is closely examined. I may say that the more closely it is examined, the more incredible it becomes.

"No one but those whom Roger Truscott left behind in that office can say what happened after he had gone, and that is something, I submit, which they have not done.

"They telephoned to the police actually *eight minutes* after Roger Truscott was seated in a restaurant five minutes' walk away. While he took that walk, and during the eight minutes that followed, we are asked to believe that Albert Menzies did nothing but run down the stairs and gaze at the dead man till his master, who also did nothing else, told him to ring up the police. It is a discrepancy which transfers a wildly improbable accusation into the realm of the utterly unbelievable. And for these reasons, in justice to my client, and still more in the public interest, so that no further time may be lost in the search for the actual murderer, which these proceedings must suspend, and for whose apprehension no one is more anxious than Roger Truscott, the brother of the young man who was so treacherously killed, I ask you to dismiss the charge."

Mr. Buxted, who had listened with an attentive but otherwise impassive countenance, now spoke in the low expressionless voice in which his decisions were most often given:

"No"—with a glance at Mr. Wedland-Wedland, obviously eager to rise—"I don't think I need call upon you further. Mr. Tonks, you have put your client's case, if you will allow me to say so, with exceptional ability, but it is obviously one for a jury's decision. Roger Truscott, I commit you to take your trial at the Central Criminal Court." He let the sentence pause as he bent over to the clerk to ascertain the date to which the committal would apply, and its conclusion was disregarded by spectators who recognised that the immediate drama was over.

CHAPTER XXII.

MR. EVANS was not able to make his report till the evening of the next day, and it was then of a somewhat negative kind.

Miss Diana Morton was a young lady of excellent character and antecedents. Her parents were dead, and she was now living with an elderly lady, a second cousin, Miss Martha Dalrymple, at 15, Cossett Drive, Lewisham.

In her position as confidential secretary to Mr. Boddington, she had the respect rather than the liking of the remainder of the staff, toward whom she maintained an attitude of friendly reserve.

She was a member of the Lewisham Tennis Club, but at this time of year her business hours rendered it impossible for her to be there except on Saturday and Sunday afternoons or evenings. On Sunday mornings she usually accompanied Miss Dalrymple to St. Innocent's Church.

Mr. Evans' enquiries led him to conclude that if she were approached on any business matter, she would be likely to refuse information, and to report to her employer what had occurred.

He had not yet been able to find that she had any intimate friend, but if this matter could be left till the end of the week, and if expense were no obstacle, something might be done at the club more profitably than in the city. There might be friendships there—even indiscreet ones—and girls will talk to one another of the matters that fill their minds. Even a new friendship might be formed with some congenial girl who had not previously been seen at the club! At the least, the subject of the murder, now discussed in every household, could be introduced in her presence, and her words and reactions noted.

Such were Mr. Evans' suggestions. Leslie said: "Thanks, but I'll let you know tomorrow if you're to go ahead on those lines. The address may be all we need."

He had considered during the day whether he should not see Mr. Boddington, and ask him directly whether he could give him any information such as would be helpful in Roger's defence. But he had hesitated on this decision, because he saw that, if Mr. Boddington were implicated in any financial irregularity which had been plotted to obtain the brothers' inheritance at an inadequate price, he would be most unlikely either to admit his delinquency or to assist in exposing his fellow conspirators.

In fact, the more willing he might be to help, the less likely it would be that there would be any help he could give. And if he had any guilty knowledge, to enquire would be to put him on his guard more vigilantly than the course of the police court defence must have done already.

On the other hand, if the position of Mr. Boddington were that of an independent auditor of the accounts of Truscott & Rowton Ltd, which must be assumed in the absence of any contrary evidence, and in any event, was what he would wish and expect that Roger's solicitors would believe, there was nothing unprofessional, nor calculated to excite reasonable suspicion, in approaching Miss Morton, if he should have reason to think that she could assist the defence. At the most, and if it should utterly fail, it could give Mr. Boddington no more warning than would be the consequence of a direct approach.

Reflecting thus, he decided to go that evening, and give Miss Morton an unexpected call.

It was 8:30 P.M. when he arrived at 15, Cossett Drive, and looked up at a house the front windows of which showed no light, though the spring dusk was closing. He went through an iron gate along a few yards of twisting gravel path, with rhododendrons growing closely on either side, and up three whitened steps to a dark-green door set in a white-plastered archway; and recognised the electric bell that he pressed as the only evidence of the present century which the dwelling showed.

He had a minute of waiting, giving him time to fear that the house might be empty and his evening lost, and had rung a second time before he heard a light quick step in the hall, and Miss Morton herself opened the door.

"Miss Morton, I believe?" he asked. "I am Leslie Tonks, of Tonks & Weatherhead. May I speak to you for a few minutes?"

She knew him, of course. There was enough light for that, even before she touched the switch in the hall, and had it been midnight darkness she would have recognised the voice of which she had heard so much during the last two days.

"Yes," she said, "come in. I am sorry you were kept waiting. The maid is out, and I happen to be alone in the house."

As she spoke she led the way to a room that was pleasantly furnished and in a more modern style than the exterior of the house suggested.

She was obviously surprised at his call, and, he thought, under a natural habit of self-control, not entirely free from nervousness as to its cause.

He felt instinctively that his approach could not be too simple, nor too direct. He said at once: "I have come to see you, Miss Morton, in the hope that you may be able to give me information which will assist in Roger Truscott's defence."

"But why, "she asked, "should you come to me?"

"Because I felt sure that you would be glad to help him, if it is in your power."

"Yes, almost anyone would. But what do you suppose I can do?"

"You must have followed the case very closely. I have noticed that you have been taking it down on both days."

"I have been taking it down for Bagley & Co., not for myself."

"It is perhaps natural that Mr. Boddington should take a special interest in the case, being the auditor to the firm."

"Yes. I suppose it is. But perhaps I ought to explain that I was doing it at my own request. Mr. Boddington often requires reports of business meetings which he attends, and this work has been done for him by Miss Smailes, who is in the general office. I suggested that, if he would let me attend this trial, it would give me an opportunity of showing that I am competent for such work."

"About which I feel sure that you have been able to satisfy him."

"Yes, I think I have."

"But as I said, you must have followed the evidence closely in taking it down, and then transcribing it. What I particularly wanted to ask you was whether you thought Mr. Rowton was telling the truth?"

"No," she said, with a deliberation that was without reluctance, "I am sure he was not."

Leslie Tonks may be excused if he thought, from that reply, that he had struck oil at last. He remembered the answer that, according to Johnny Pember's very reliable observation, she had received with a glance of incredulity. "I suppose," he said, "that would apply to his assurance that he had no prior knowledge regarding the Brazilian contract?"

But he found that the question was ill-received. He was aware of a new reserve in her voice, as well as of the fact that it was left unanswered, as she replied: "I thought you were asking about the murder."

"So I was. Both. Of course, the murder's the more important. If you can tell me anything directly bearing on that—"

"I'm sorry I can't. I wish I could. I feel sure that Mr. Rowton was lying, and, of course, Menzies as well. I'm not sure about the porter. I believe Roger Truscott. But that's only what I think. I don't know anything about it myself."

"I am sorry for that. I had an idea that you might have helped us more. But even if you can put me on anything that will show that Rowton's been playing a double game in financial matters, it might help."

"I don't think you should ask me questions of that kind."

"Why not? Do you mean that I should address them to Mr. Boddington? Do you think he will give me the information better? You surely would not imply that if Rowton hasn't been going straight, he would wish it to be concealed, especially now? What is an auditor for?"

"I can't answer questions like that."

"But you know he knows?"

"I have not said so. I have not said anything about it."

"But you have not denied it, which is the same thing."

"How can I tell what he would say? Mr. Tonks, do you think you are being quite fair?"

"I didn't intend to be otherwise. But do you recognise that a man's life is at stake?"

He thought she lost colour at that. "You can't mean that seriously," she said. "Not about the contract, anyway." And then, in a more earnest tone: "You don't really mean that there's any doubt that you'll get him off?"

"There's a real doubt, if we don't get more information than we have now. But I don't intend to fail about that. Miss Morton," he added earnestly, "I think I see how you are placed, and perhaps I can get some things that I want in another way without worrying you. But I ask your promise for this, that if you should learn the truth of who shot Cyril Truscott, or anything that will help to prove Roger's innocence, you will not let *any scruple of any kind* stand in the way of letting me know at once."

"Yes," she said, after a moment's pause, with the same conscious deliberation as before, "you can be quite sure of that." And then, after another pause: "Shall you see Mr. Boddington now?"

"Yes, I expect I shall. Why?"

"Shall you mention that you have seen me?"

"Probably not. I must use my own judgement. Why?"

"I don't think I should."

"Shouldn't what? See Boddington, or tell him that I've seen you?"

"I don't think I should do either."

"I don't pledge myself, but I am disposed to trust your promise and take your advice."

"I'm afraid I can't leave it like that. I must tell Mr. Boddington, unless you are quite clear."

"You mean unless I pledge myself not to discuss it with Mr. Boddington, you will tell him that I've been here tonight?"

"Yes."

"But if I do, you won't mention it to him?"

"Yes."

"Then I agree to that, and shall hope to hear from you. You know you can get through to me at the office at any time."

"You mustn't expect anything. You had better go now. My cousin may be coming in."

Leslie went at that. She shook hands, and led him to the door with troubled, unsmiling eyes, but he went away feeling that he had gained an ally.

CHAPTER XXIII.

THE interview with Miss Morton had the effect of raising the spirits of Roger Truscott's solicitor somewhat beyond what he could himself regard as a logical consequence. She had denied knowledge of anything which would throw light on the murder itself, and though there had been an implication that she judged Ellis Rowton with duplicity over the Brazilian contract, she had refused to communicate any reason that she might have to support that opinion. The promise she had given was vague and conditional, and, indeed, "given" was scarcely the right word to apply, for she had rather sold it, problematical as its value might be, for an immediate payment in the form of his promise that he would not acquaint Mr. Boddington of his call upon her.

Considering these facts, he went next morning into his partner's office to take counsel upon it, as his custom was, and to observe its effect on another mind.

"That's how it worked," he concluded, when he had narrated the conversation of the previous night. "You may say I have drawn a blank. The question is: what to do next?"

"I shouldn't say that," Mr. Weatherhead replied in as hopeful a tone as he would often use. "I think you have some cause to be satisfied. It's something to find that someone who has observed the case rather closely and may have had opportunities of overhearing things that she doesn't feel free to speak, is convinced that Roger is innocent. It's strong support for your belief—which I have come to share much more than I did at first—that he has told no less than the truth; and that's really the most important point of all, for I needn't tell you that we've got a far better chance of breaking down the witnesses' tales if they are untrue, than if they are no worse than the truth being told in a clumsy way, or some error of clocks seeming to give you a better case than you ought to have.

"Beyond that, I think the young lady was right. She's in Bagley's employment now, and if she knows matters which may be confidential about the firm's clients, she has no business to discuss them, even with us.

"Of course, we ought to be told, but it's Boddington's place, not hers, to do that; and she may have no more than a doubtful guess that that isn't just what he means to do.

"But if there's something more serious being concealed, whether Boddington's in it or not (which is a rather wild supposition), if she learns anything that ought to come out—I mean as to the murder itself—she doesn't regard the terms of her employment as covering that, and if no one else speaks, she will.

"That's what I understand her to mean, and I suppose you'll agree that she's more likely to learn something—supposing there's anything that can be learned in that quarter—while she's still employed, than if she were under suspicion, and shown the door with a month's salary in her hand."

"Then you'd just leave things alone in that direction?"

"Yes, as far as Miss Morton is concerned, I certainly should. For the next fortnight, at least. If we've heard nothing from her by then, and made no progress in other directions, it might be time for another talk. But as to Boddington, I don't know. We ought to be able to rely on any help he can give, though I don't know quite what we can expect it to be."

"He's always been friendly with Rowton."

"Yes, but in no more than a business way. Rowton has been an important client to him. I shouldn't say he's a man who lets friendship influence him much in business affairs."

"He was very keen on getting that deed signed, when Roger Truscott jibbed."

"Yes, I noticed that. So were we at first. It may have been genuine enough."

"But I don't think it was. If we were giving the same advice, it was mainly on what we had been told by Rowton, and Boddington himself. An auditor knows a lot that we don't, or we take it on trust from him."

"And so, adding Miss Morton's significant reticence, you think that Rowton plotted to rob the young Truscotts, and Boddington was probably in the game?"

"Yes. I think that. Or if Boddington didn't know at first—if Rowton made him a cat's-paw, as he tried to make us—I think he knows now."

"Then you ought to see him, and make up your mind which it is. In any case, if he has done something disreputable financially—or tried to do it—it doesn't follow that he's got any sympathy with murder. He might be willing to help us there—though I can't see what kind of help it's likely to be."

"Well, I'll give him a call. But I thought of seeing Inspector Byfleet first."

"What do you hope to get there?"

"I want to shake his belief in Roger's guilt, if I can. I want to ask his help in still trying to get at the truth. There are things the police can do that we can't, and we want every bit of help from every quarter that we're likely to get."

"It's a good deal to ask. But I've always found the police very fair, if they're approached in the right way. I don't say you're wrong to try. But there's something come by the morning post that you ought to see. I was only keeping it till we'd finished with what was on your mind already. "

As he spoke, he passed over a blue envelope of a cheap type, which had come with the morning's post, the firm's address being in block capitals, made with clumsiness of a deliberate kind.

Leslie drew a similar sheet of paper from the envelope, and read:

ROGER CAME OUT FIRST. I KNOW THAT FOR I SAW. STICK TO THAT AND YOU WILL COME OUT RIGHT IN THE END. I DON'T KNOW MORE. I WISH I DID. IF I FIND OUT I SHALL LET YOU KNOW.

There was no signature, no address, no date. The envelope bore an E.C. postmark. The paper and envelope might have been bought anywhere.

"Probably quite valueless, and quite likely a hoax," Mr. Weatherhead said; "but you never know."

"It's not exactly a hoax," Leslie replied, "because I'm practically sure it's the same paper and the same writing as a similar note that was put on Roger's desk telling him not to give way about selling the shares. It's someone on the premises there who's afraid to speak out. I've got the first note in my desk now."

He fetched it from his own room, and there was no difficulty in agreeing that the two notes were written by the same hand.

"I think," Leslie said, "I'll show Byfleet this. I'll go now, if he's in."

Five minutes later he had learnt that Inspector Byfleet would see him if he could be at Scotland Yard within the next hour, and ten minutes after that he was shaking hands with the Inspector, who received him cordially in one of the more private rooms which is reserved for such interviews.

"I suppose," he said, "you've come to see me about the Truscott murder, and before you begin, whatever you've got now, I should like to say that I never saw a better fight put up in a hopeless case. We're all agreed about that. And I'll go further, and say that you've shaken up the case more than I thought anything could. The Sub-Commissioner's been quite worried as to whether there isn't something fishy about the evidence we've put up. And if you ask me, and it's only between ourselves, I should say there aren't many lies that Mr. Rowton wouldn't tell for a good cheque, and Menzies the same, though his price might be a bit less. But I'll say we've got the right man all the same, and you won't do him any good by showing that Rowton wanted to fleece him over the deal, as I've no doubt that he did...and after all, you know, they weren't trying to skin them clean. They were going to give them thirty thousand pounds, and you can't say that that isn't a tidy picking, even if it's off a big bone."

"Inspector, you don't want to hang an innocent man?"

"No, you're right there. It's something we don't want, and we don't do."

"Well, I tell you I'm certain that Roger Truscott never shot his brother. I don't say it because I'm his lawyer. I say it as man to man, and I ask your help so that the truth may be brought to light."

"We can't blow hot and cold. We say we've got our man now. If you say we're wrong, can you give me a better guess? Motive, opportunity, almost seen in the act. Tell me anyone else who fills the bill in that way, and I'll listen as hard as I can."

"That's what I want you to help me in finding out."

"And I say you can't find a man who was never there."

"You can't say that your case is as clear as you like to have them. You haven't traced the gun yet."

"No, and I daresay we never shall. It's too common a pattern among those that were brought here after the war."

"But you would have done, if Roger had bought it, as you suppose that he had."

"Well, I'll give you that. We should be glad to trace that gun, and there's lots of time yet."

"And I hope you'll succeed. Then there's that curious difference about the time, which they'd got no explanation ready to meet."

"Yes. I'll give you that too. It's a bit long for them to have stood gazing with their mouths open at the dead man. But where does it lead, and how far? Suppose they hesitated what to do? Suppose they thought of leaving the body there till someone found it when he came up? Suppose what you like. It doesn't alter the fact that you've got three men telling the same tale, and not even a suggestion to make of what happened if it's all lies."

He took a more serious tone as he concluded: "Mr. Tonks, I can assure you we've looked at this from every angle there is. It isn't only myself. We've had it looked over by all the best brains in the Yard. We've said 'Suppose Rowton did it himself?' But why should he? We can't discover that he had any reason on earth. We can't find that he had a gun, or ever handled one in his life. It's the same with Menzies. And why should he, again? We've even thought of Bellman. He does know how to shoot! But suppose Bellman went suddenly mad, and shot a man on the private stairs that he scarcely knew, would Rowton and Menzies both risk a ten years' sentence to save his neck, and put the rope round the neck of another man? Porters aren't usually loved quite so dearly as that, even when any homicidal tendencies they may possess are under rather better control."

"Yes. I see how it looks. But something did happen in that interval, all the same—something we haven't found out, and can't guess—and if it comes out at last, I suppose there are two points on which you'd agree with me: that it would be better for it to come out before it's too late—I mean before Roger Truscott's hanged for a crime he didn't commit; and that it should be the police who make the discovery which must set him free."

Inspector Byfleet did not dissent from either of these propositions. He received them with a good-humoured smile, which suggested that he could contemplate them without loss of sleep. "What," he asked, "do you want us to do?"

"I want you to go on probing what happened in the office after Roger left at five past one, as we know he did, and to find the man who possessed that gun."

"We're doing both those things now. We'd always rather not have any loose ends in a case like this. I'll go further than that. If you can bring us any fresh facts, we'll go into them without asking where we shall end up. You can't ask us for more than that."

"No. I don't think I could. Perhaps you'd like to look at these notes?"

He spread out the two anonymous letters, and the Inspector gazed upon them with a mental shrug which he would not show. He had seen so many of such communications before. And almost every one had proved to be either a hoax, or a trick to draw suspicion away from a guilty man.

He was roused to a somewhat livelier interest when he learnt how Roger had received the first, and inspected them with a closer regard.

"Someone on the staff, no doubt; and he seems to have been friendly to Roger, and given him good advice at the first attempt. Now he's trying to help him again. But if it's true that he saw him go out first, why doesn't he come forward properly? He'd have nothing to fear."

"Not knowing the man, I can't say. But thought that it ought to be possible to find him, if he's on the staff; and I didn't think Rowton was the right man to ask for help. I thought you'd do it best, and I'd rather trust you than him."

"You mean to leave these letters with us?"

"That was what I thought."

Inspector Byfleet looked speculatively at Roger Truscott's solicitor. "You say you'd rather trust us, than Rowton. I don't say you're wrong about that. I'll follow these up, and I shall be very glad to have a few words with the man who wrote them. If you find they have damned your case rather than helped it, you mustn't blame me."

"I think I'll risk that."

Leslie rose to go as he spoke. They shook hands very cordially, and as he went out through the door, the Inspector's voice followed him: "If Roger Truscott's innocent, which I don't believe, you can tell him he's got nothing to fear. We don't hang innocent men."

Leslie wished that he could be equally sure about that.

CHAPTER XXIV.

LESLIE left Inspector Byfleet with a feeling that he had not wasted his time. He knew that the police would trace the writer of those anonymous letters with more speed and certainty than he would have hoped to do without Mr. Rowton's aid, which he would not have cared to ask; nor could he have felt any confidence that it would have been honestly given. Whether or not his evidence regarding the murder had been genuine—which it was hard to believe—he was sure that Mr. Rowton was well content that Roger should stand in a felon's dock. Indeed, however much or little responsibility he might have for prior events, it was scarcely within the limits of human nature that he should feel otherwise at the stage which they had now reached. Cyril dead and Roger released would mean that Roger would have entire and lasting control over the business which Ellis Rowton had ruled for seventeen years. And, after what had now happened, it was unlikely that they could work together on any terms.

So it was much the better course that the police should be asked to search for the author of those anonymous letters. And Leslie was well content to think that he had left Inspector Byfleet, in spite of the confidence of his demeanour, just a little shaken in his belief that there was no question of Roger's guilt.

But, however cheerful he might feel, he did not conceal from himself that the core of the problem was still unreached, and the hours passed. He thought of Roger in the solitude of his cell, or taking exercise when and for how long he was told, in that regulated physical slavery of the modern prison—of Roger waiting, as the fatal hours went by, for the news which he could not take; and he felt that something more must be tried before the sun should set on another day.

Rowton might be hostile—there was clear reason for that—but there was no more than an instinct of distrust to warn him that Boddington might be of a kindred mood. Bagley & Co. had apparently

139

nothing but a good audit either to hold or lose. They had done all they could to support Mr. Rowton's policy, and if Roger's life should end in the hangman's shed, they could have no fear that they would be disturbed in the office they held. On the other hand, if Roger should be acquitted, he would have power to terminate their position. It might seem an obvious policy to act in such a way now as to convince him of their past integrity, and, if possible, to place him under such obligations as he could not lightly forget.

And, apart from such arguments, there was the rule of professional etiquette, of professional honour, which it was not right to suppose they would disregard; and it might seem that, at such an issue as this, all smaller considerations should be forgotten.

As he considered thus and remembered his partner's advice, it became clear to Leslie that he must see Mr. Boddington. It was still slightly before noon when he got back to his office, and he rang up the accountant at once.

Mr. Boddington said that he already had a very full day, but he would like an opportunity to talk things over with Mr. Tonks. To-morrow? Yes, that would do. But what about lunch today? Bradings? He didn't mind. But the Sphinx was often less crowded. What about that?

Leslie agreed, with a mental observation that Mr. Boddington was, at least, indifferent to whether Mr. Rowton should know that they had come together, for the Sphinx was Ellis Rowton's favourite midday resort.

One o'clock, or perhaps five minutes past? Yes, that would do. So it came that the two gentlemen were seated opposite one another within an hour at a table for two in a retired alcove of the Sphinx restaurant, and Mr. Boddington, losing no time in coming to that which was in both their minds, commenced the conversation by saying: "I thought it best not to mention it on the telephone, but I suppose you wanted to have a talk about this dreadful Truscott affair."

"Yes. I wondered if you could help me in any way."

"I should be glad to, of course. Considering how you must have been hampered by your instructions, you did rather well at the committal. At least, that's what everyone's saying. I wasn't there myself."

"I can't honestly say that I was hampered by my instructions. It was Roger's own line of defence, but it had our entire approval."

Mr. Boddington looked mildly surprised.

"Well, of course you know best about that. I only mentioned what seems to have been the general impression among those who were looking on."

Leslie was inwardly somewhat disconcerted by this observation. Was it true that those who listened had considered Roger's denial to be as futile as it had first sounded to him, that his inexperience in such advocacy had led him into an error which would be the loss of his client's life? Even so, the blame was not his. It was Roger who had insisted on that defence.

Mr. Boddington looked at him with shrewdly observant eyes, as he added: "I should say you'll find counsel will insist on a different line. That is, if you're briefing one of the big names. They won't let any murderer make them look like a public fool. It wouldn't pay them to, not for a four-figure brief."

"But suppose it's the true defence?"

"Well, we happen to know it isn't. Rowton was lunching with me here yesterday. He says that Roger followed out almost at Cyril's back. He thought he heard a moment's quarrelling on the stairs, and then came the shot, and Menzies went to the door at once. He was surprised that Roger got down as far as he did. He didn't tell it quite like that in the witness box. He didn't want to make it worse than he must, and he said he wished Menzies hadn't been so sure that it was Roger he saw at the foot of the stairs. He doesn't want the young fool to hang. But, speaking between ourselves, there isn't the faintest doubt of how Cyril was shot, or who by. Couldn't you do something on the insanity line?"

"You feel you can trust anything Rowton says?"

"In a matter like this, yes. I don't say he couldn't tell a good thumping lie in a business deal. But he's straight enough about this. More or less, he couldn't help telling the truth, Cyril being shot where he was, and Roger just gone out of the door. Besides, Menzies is the worst witness for you. He saw more than Rowton, and Rowton only corroborates."

Leslie went on with his lunch, in no hurry to continue a conversation which was not developing on the lines he had intended. He thought that, whether Rowton were telling the truth or not, he had convinced his accountant of his veracity on this occasion, though that gentleman was aware, as he had stated bluntly enough, that truth and Ellis Rowton were not constant companions.

Mr. Boddington broke the silence to say again: "It's insanity I suggest, as the one plea that gives you a fighting chance. It's not for me to dictate, but you ask my opinion, and I say that's the only defence. I venture to say that if you don't work it up in that way, in two months from now Roger Truscott will be a dead man."

"I don't see how we could. Roger's as sane as a man can be."

"I daresay he is, but that doesn't matter if you can bring a doubt to the right minds. Why not get a couple of good alienists on it at once? Obsession from childhood of carrying out the parental wishes. Business must be maintained at all costs, as his father planned. Suddenly, it seems that all the world is combined to thwart him, just at the moment when he thought he had come to power. Strongest of all, and most violent, is his brother's attitude. Final quarrel produces a moment of emotional insanity. They'd call it brainstorm in the States, and have him out of jail in a week. Of course, it wouldn't follow that he isn't sane now. Well, think it over. It's a straight tip. You won't get on very well with no more to say than that he swears that he wasn't there. There wouldn't be many murderers hanged, if that was a way out."

Leslie saw that it was no use saying more concerning the murder itself. It seemed that Mr. Boddington's mind was made up, and he let the subject drop without troubling as to whether or not he appeared to have been converted to the idea as a possible defence, in which it seemed that the accountant had more faith than he could easily feel.

"What I really wanted to ask you," he said, "was about this Brazilian contract, and the question of the sale of the business. It's a minor matter, but I don't know how far it may lead us on. Did Rowton know all the time, and if so, why did he want Lessings to get the shares? On the face of it, it was just as much to his interest as to Roger's to hold on. I know there are ways of finding out where a contract will be placed, sometimes a good while before any official announcement comes through."

"Yes. I should say there are. But don't see why Rowton shouldn't have run straight this time. As you say, his interests and Roger Truscott's were very much the same. But isn't the only practical question what you're going to do now? It can't be to Roger's interests to keep the shares as he's placed now. He'll need funds for his defence, and if you think Rowton's a rogue (which may be coming it a bit strong), it's all the more important to sell out of a business which he—I mean Roger—can't hope to control (even if he gets off with a lifer) for fifteen years."

"I thought the date of the final offer expired?"

"So it did; but I shouldn't worry over that. Now that T. & R. have got the Brazilian order, you can be sure that Lessings will be more keen to buy than they were before. The only trouble is that, with one brother dead, and the other likely to hang in a few weeks, they may think that we're forced to sell. But I should stand out for a bit higher price all the same. Why not let me see how high I can get them to go, and give me power to close the deal at the best price I can get, providing it's an advance on the five shillings a share that they offered before?"

"I couldn't agree that without my client's instructions. We should probably want written ones before we should be willing to do anything in the present circumstances."

"Yes, of course, but it's for you to decide. He's in your hands, and he's come to the point where he'll be glad to do as he's told, if he doesn't want to lose the last friend that he's got left in the world."

"Well, I'll take his instructions. There'll be no harm in you sounding Lessings again. But I should say the price ought to be nearer fifteen shillings than five."

Mr. Boddington shook his head doubtfully. "They won't go to anything like that. Not in the present position. But I'll raise them the most I can."

Mr. Boddington looked at the clock as he said this. He remarked that he had to be at a Frost and Hatchett's meeting in twenty minutes, and that he must look in at his own office before then. He called hurriedly for the bill.

They parted with some cordiality, each having a comfortable conviction that he had misled the other, and each being partly right, if not more.

Leslie, conscious that he was still in the dark concerning several things he would like to know, was determined to give no confidence to anyone who professed conviction of Roger's guilt. He did not mean to press Roger to sell the shares, at whatever price, but there could be no harm in letting Boddington enquire what they would fetch now, as he had himself proposed it. It might be interesting to learn what he would consider a satisfactory price.

Mr. Boddington was equally satisfied. He was confident that, whatever suspicions the solicitor might have of Ellis Rowton, he did not attach them to himself, and he thought that he had inoculated him with the idea of temporary insanity as the most hopeful line of defence in such a manner that it would be likely to grow as the days passed. That was the best defence in every way from his point of view. Its adoption would be the end of any further probing of the little discrepancy of time, which Mr. Boddington thought could lead to no good, and might produce, from his standpoint, a good deal of harm; and it was probably the best channel of escaping the rope that Roger Truscott had, about which Mr. Boddington was not entirely indifferent, though he had too many things of greater personal urgency on his mind to care much about that, one way or other, so long as his own schemes should prevail.

He hurried back to his office, somewhat to Miss Morton's surprise, for he had told her that he should not return after lunch, and she knew that his time was short, but he found her working with her usual diligence, as he would have expected to do.

"Miss Morton," he said rather hurriedly, "I want you to phone Mr. Rowton in about half an hour from now. It's no use ringing up yet. I know he wouldn't be in. He was taking a customer out to lunch. He was to have him on his hands all day till the 4:05 from Paddington. Tell him I'd have spoken myself, but I've got an appointment I can't break. I want him to be round here at 4:45. Tell him I've had lunch with Tonks, talking over the Truscott affair. He mustn't fail to be here."

He started out as he concluded these instructions, and then turned back to ask: "You haven't very much on hand this afternoon, have you?"

"Yes, I've got the Sperryn report and accounts and I haven't started your letters yet. I don't expect to be through much before seven."

"You'd better leave the Sperryn papers just as they are. There's something I want to look at again before the report goes up to Sir Peter. Just get through the letters, and you needn't wait if I'm not back. I expect a few hours of tennis will do you good." He was gone before she had time to reply.

She became thoughtful after he left. She did not believe that the Sperryn accounts needed any further revision, nor that Mr. Boddington's instructions were based on the idea that she ought to have more time for sports. He wanted a vacant office when the head of Truscott & Rowton should call upon him. That had happened before—but why?

It was not a matter for resentment, nor would even curiosity have been normally creditable. A man has a right to privacy in his own office. He has a right to limit his confidence in the best of secretaries. And, so far as she has his confidence, she must still respect it, though it does not go all the way.

The trouble on her mind was that in this Truscott affair it did go all the way—or, at least, what should surely be the whole distance. If she could not say that he had told her his plans—he never did that about anything—he did not conceal anything from her. She might observe or infer what she would. He relied upon her intelligence to understand what was going on sufficiently well to carry out his instructions without blundering, and upon her honour not to use it for her own purposes or reveal it to others.

Even now, he was making no secrecy of the fact that he wanted Mr. Rowton to come to him, nor that it was a sudden decision, following something that had occurred at his lunchtime interview with Roger Truscott's solicitor. She was to arrange the appointment—but she was not to be there. The fact would have been less remarkable had he ever acted in the same way in regard to other interviews, but its only parallel was the previous instance in which Ellis Rowton had been concerned.

She thought of it as she typed Mr. Boddington's letters, which were not many, and she thought of the interview she had had with Mr. Tonks the night before, and the promise she had given. But, most of all, the memory would recur of a time when Roger Truscott's eyes had met hers as he stood in a felon's dock, and it had seemed to her that they protested his innocence, and she knew that her own eyes had answered that she believed.

She believed still. Yet even his own lawyer said that he might be condemned to death unless more evidence could be obtained. And if he were innocent, was it not almost certain that they must know things that they had not chosen to say?

And her own employer—was he not at least so far involved that he had been plotting with Rowton to rob the two youths whose interests they were bound in honour to protect? She did not know enough of the facts, nor of the law on such matters, to judge whether there had been explicit criminality in what they had attempted to do, but of its moral baseness she could not doubt. She remembered that cable, with its single revealing word. She had a conviction that if she could overhear the interview which she had just arranged, she would know more of how Cyril Truscott died. And as she thought of that, an idea came, and was thrust aside.

It was about 3:45 when the letters were finished, and placed upon Mr. Boddington's desk for his signature by the side of some private ones which had come in by the afternoon post, and including one which she knew to be from his stockbrokers, which had been delivered by hand an hour ago. She hesitated, and went back to her own seat.

The window frames in that ancient room were ill-fitting, and Mr. Boddington complained of a draught when the wind came from the east or north. At such times, he would have a folding screen placed between his desk and the window in the east wall.

At others it would be moved backward, letting the light in. The light was not much at the best. Mr. Boddington usually worked with an electric light over his desk if the day were dull (as it was now). She had a table lamp on her own, which she used constantly to throw its light on the notebook or documents from which she copied.

She walked over to the screen. It was almost flat against the wall for the length of two sections. The third was bent somewhat forward to enable it to stand upright. There was space—barely space—for her to stand between it and the wall.

She did not really mean to do it. Every instinct and habit revolted against the idea. But if a man's life…? She did not think of it in that impersonal way. If Roger Truscott's life—

Suppose, she thought, she were to listen with the resolution that she would make no mention of what she heard, even though it were a plot to rob Roger Truscott of the last penny he had, so long as the conversation went no further than financial matters, which were part of the business of the man in whose employment she was. Even though she might decide to resign at once, she would make no use of anything which had been learned in so base a way. Only if there should be something which it was vital for Roger's lawyers to know for his life's defence would she speak, be the consequences what they might.

Yet she still felt that she did no more than toy with the thought—that it was something she could not do. Suppose she were discovered? Suppose Mr. Boddington always looked behind the screen when he wished for a certain solitude? She would be dismissed without notice and without character. It was no slight risk, even in that aspect.

But then she asked herself, was it honour or cowardice that held her back? Suppose Roger should be hanged (but that was too dreadful to think) because she had lacked the courage to do what she knew she ought?

She walked over to the screen again. The space was very narrow. Suppose she should pull it out just an inch or two? But she resisted the inclination. It would be to increase the chance of it catching Mr. Boddington's eyes—of the look behind which would ruin all.

And as she stood thus, she knew the answer to the question she had asked herself. It was cowardice, not nobility of character which was holding her back. And as she realised this she walked deliberately to her own desk and put out the light upon it. She covered up the typewriter. She made other little adjustments which would imply that she had finished and gone.

Mr. Boddington might be here any minute now. Here, in fact, he was. She could hear his voice giving a curt admonition to one of the staff. She stepped quietly behind the screen.

146

Suppose he asked whether she had left? But it was not likely he would. He would come in prepared to send her away, or would accept the fact of the darkened and vacant room. The position was very cramped. She wished she had moved the screen, if only an inch. It was not too late now. How she hated it, and herself. It was not too late to give it up, even now.

But as she hesitated whether to move the screen, or to give up the idea, Mr. Boddington entered the room.

CHAPTER XXV.

SHE heard him go to his desk with his usual quick step. He switched on the light, though it was broad daylight outside. The action revealed to her that she could see somewhat, as well as hear. The screen was a loose fit at the hinge, and the lining was somewhat slit. She could see Mr. Boddington's hand among the letters. It was only a narrow view.

He read them over, and signed them. He rang for Stubbs to take them out. It seemed that it must be past the time at which Ellis Rowton should be there, but he did not come.

Mr. Boddington got up from his chair. He began to pace the room. If he came too far—but the danger passed, for Mr. Rowton was announced.

She heard their greeting, and knew that there was no love between the two men. Freed from the restraint of observers, Mr. Boddington's voice was hard, and Mr. Rowton's sullen. He sat down—Diana could hear the accountant closing and locking his double door. She had a moment of panic. Suppose she should be discovered after she had heard some secret they could not afford to risk? She would be utterly in their power. Even her life might be the price they would make her pay.

The fear brought its own courage; and it seemed that there was no present probability that she would be discovered if she remained still. The two men were seated now, and Mr. Boddington was speaking with little regard for the ordinary amenities of a business interview.

"I saw Tonks today, and it looks as though I've got you another chance."

Ellis Rowton's voice showed no gratitude as he enquired: "What is it now?"

"I learnt, in the first place, that he knows no more than he did when he took the case."

"You can't always tell what he knows."

"But you can tell what he doesn't. He made that appointment, not I. He came to me for information he didn't get, and he had to turn his cards up. For one thing, he wants to know whether Lessings are still willing to buy."

"Did he say that?"

"Not at first. He let the advice come from me. He said he didn't trust you, and I told him that, if he were right there, it was an extra reason to sell, for you'd have a free hand with everything now that Roger Truscott's put where he is."

"Then he isn't hoping to get him off?"

"He's where he was about that. Harping on the question of the time when you rang up, and thinking he ought to be able to make something of that, though he can't tell what. I don't pretend to know why you didn't ring sooner, and I don't suppose I ever shall; but as a defence for Truscott I told him it was too thin. I told him no decent counsel would take the brief. Insanity's his chance, and I rubbed it in."

"You think he'll defend on that ground?"

"I think he'll stop saying that his man wasn't there, and then what has he got left? But I didn't send for you to tell you this."

"No," the answer came resentfully, "you wouldn't have troubled."

"And why should I? But see here, Rowton, you'd better stop taking that tone with me. I've had more than enough. You can phone Lessings' solicitors in the morning, and give them a hint that you think the sale's still possible, but say that it won't do for you to move, as you know that Tonks wouldn't take it the right way. Tell them the best chance is for them to make some excuse to phone me, and bring up the subject themselves. Tell them they may have to spring the price a bit, now that this contract's placed, but advise them to try a small advance first. Say what you like beyond that, but don't seem to know too much. And, look here, Rowton"—with a sudden, sharp change of tone—"I've got to have two thousand to-morrow."

As Mr. Boddington had been talking, he had opened the letter before him. Diana Morton could see this, though she could not see the face of either man. She saw his hand on the desk, and she had seen that he had retained one of the letters in it, which she thought she knew to be that which had been delivered an hour ago.

"You can't have that. It isn't possible."

"I'm afraid it's got to be possible. And in cash, too."

"And I tell you it can't be done. Why didn't you give me longer notice?"

"Because I only knew when I opened this letter. But the money I've got to have. You'll find a way to bring it here by twelve, if you're a wise man, as I think you are."

"Why by twelve? Wouldn't after lunch do?"

"No, it won't, after what you said. It's a matter on which I can't fail, and I don't intend running any risk trusting to you. If it's not here by twelve, I shall get it another way, and if I have to do that, you can put a bullet through your head as the best way out."

"You seem to forget that we're in the same boat."

"No, I don't. The boat's all right, and I mean it to come to land; but I don't know whether you'll be in it when it does. That's for you to decide."

"You know, Boddington, there's such a thing as bluffing a bit too high."

"So there is, and you'll find it's no use to try it on me. Now listen, Rowton. You're no fool. Just listen, and think it out. Suppose the things that have happened the last few weeks have made the auditors of Truscott & Rowton just a little suspicious, and just a little worried as to whether anything may have been hidden from them that they ought to have spotted before now. You know what the responsibilities of auditors are, and it's a very natural feeling for us to have. And suppose that leads to our giving the accounts for the past ten years a few tests that we hadn't felt necessary to do before, though perhaps we ought, because we felt such confidence in the man who controlled the finances. And suppose the result should be such as to raise very grave doubts in our minds—what do you think we should do then?"

"You'd never dare try such a dirty game. Why you'd—"

"I didn't ask you that. It would be a very proper course for us to take, and the answer is that we should go to the firm's solicitors, and communicate the position to them. It would show courage as well as probity on our part, for, in a sense, we should be accusing ourselves—of negligence, if no more."

"Do you suppose I should let you do that without hitting back?"

"You might try, but what could you do?"

"Why, of course, I—What about all the money you've had from me—even in the last month?"

"It might be just that which roused our suspicions. I mean the fact that you have had so much cash to invest during the years that the business has done so poorly. Perhaps I oughtn't to tell you this, but every penny I've had is openly entered on our books. There's nothing to hide here."

"And you think I should let you get off with that? Boddington, you must be mad."

"I don't see how you could help it. To begin with, you couldn't accuse us without pleading guilty yourself, not only to the charge you might have to meet, but to a lot more. You'd have to plead guilty to embezzlement, and add conspiracy and a few other details that we couldn't suggest. You'd just turn two or three years' retirement into seven or ten. That is, if you were believed. It's more likely that it would be regarded as no more than the spite of a discredited man against those who had found him out. It wouldn't make the sentence any lighter, even then."

"Boddington, you're a heartless devil. I've learnt that since you found me out six years ago. But you can't make me believe that you'd start such trouble as that."

"It might be the safest way."

"Not with this Cyril Truscott affair on the top of everything else."

"What on earth is there in that to affect me?"

"There'd be three witnesses, if you come to that."

"Witnesses of what? Ask Menzies if he'll oblige you by going into court to swear that he's perjured himself, and see whether he'll look pleased. And what would the tale be then? They'd come out with something that no one would believe in a thousand years, and end up with the rope round their own necks, and the satisfaction of knowing that they'd put it there to oblige you. I used to think you had a business head."

"It sounds clever enough, when you put it like that. But I still say that it's a stench that you won't stir."

"If you feel sure of that, you can test it by noon tomorrow; but you can't say that you weren't warned. I'm sorry I've had to say this, and I don't want you to take it the wrong way. And if you think this is a kind of blackmail, you're quite wrong. We'll keep to the figures we first agreed, and everything will be brought into account to the last pound. But the fact is that I can't help myself. You know something of the hole I've been filling up, and I reckoned when that boy came of age that there'd be fifteen thousand to pick up in a few days, more or less, as I suppose that there will now. But I could have carried on well enough if the bottom hadn't dropped out of the market a month ago."

"If I could do this, would it be the last, or shall you be asking for more in a week's time?"

"I shan't need anything further. You can sleep easy on that."

"Well, if I can, I suppose it will be the same in the end, but if you think you've bluffed me with that talk...."

"I haven't bluffed you at all. And I know you can. Haven't you been putting money away for the last ten years, so that you could hold your own in this deal when the chance came?"

"Yes, but it's the time."

"You'll find a way to get over that. And don't forget to phone in the morning about the shares."

Diana heard him push back his chair and rise as he said this. He added: "If I'm quick, I've just got time for the seven-three."

CHAPTER XXVI.

DIANA heard the doors closed and locked as the two men passed out. She waited a few moments, against the remote chance that they might have found occasion to return, and then followed. The doors opened from the inside without difficulty, and she had her own keys. She went down past the offices of other firms on the lower floors, with a feeling that she had already escaped from the worst ordeal her life had known, which faltered a moment as she imagined Mr. Boddington unexpectedly returning, and meeting her on those narrow stairs. What excuse could she make for her presence there? Even if she had the will for a lie, she had no confidence in herself that she could succeed in an art which she did not use. But she met no one till she came out, and was at the corner of Duckling Street when she almost collided with Teddy Watts.

"Hallo," he said, with a familiarity which he affected the more because he knew it to be unwelcome, "been at it late again?"

She had the presence of mind to answer: "Have I? I hardly know what the time is," and passed on with a new thought to confuse her mind. She had come down the stairs debating whether she had a duty which overrode that of her employment, and how far it required her to reveal what she had heard in so base a way. She had doubted whether she would enter those doors again, but she had supposed that it was only at the bar of her own conscience that the decision would be made. She saw now that if Teddy had the slightest suspicion (which was unlikely), or if he should casually mention the time when she had left the office, and it should come to Mr. Boddington's hearing, she might be asked for an explanation it would not be easy to give. It was an improbable imagination, but it may have tipped the scale in a doubtful mind, and caused her to get on a Waterloo bus, instead of one which would have taken her to her own home.

She knew that Mr. Tonks lived at Surbiton, and she supposed correctly that she would have no difficulty in finding him with the aid of a telephone directory.

She was right in that, but she had a walk of nearly a mile, for Leslie Tonks did not live in one of the new Surbiton villas which have arisen in hundreds around the railway station. His father had lived there a generation ago, and now the old house, still lurking resentfully in its own seclusion, had become his.

She soon found herself waiting in a pleasant library, with the noises of an adjoining room, heard through a half-opened door, announcing that she had arrived before the hour of dinner was past. But she had only waited a few minutes when Leslie Tonks entered the room—and now that the moment she sought had come, she became aware of the treachery of that which she was about to do, and found it hard to begin.

"I hope," she said, "I haven't interrupted you at an inconvenient time."

He observed no signs of the disquiet which lay beneath her habitual self-control as he answered truthfully: "Well, we had a couple of friends come in for a game of bridge, and I don't want to be absent too long, but I'm sure you wouldn't come to see me without good reason."

"I don't know," she said doubtfully. "I think I want your advice first. I overheard something this evening which makes it seem sure that Roger Truscott is innocent. But I didn't doubt that before, and that's about as far as it went."

"Wait a moment, please," he said, and went out of the room. He returned a moment later, saying: "I've just said that they must count me out for tonight, so you'll understand that there's no hurry at all. What was it you overheard?"

"I'm not sure that I ought to repeat it all, and what I promised you, standing alone, doesn't seem to go very far."

"Suppose you tell me in confidence, and let me judge."

"I think that's asking too much."

"I suppose the difficulty is that you overheard this in the course of your employment?"

"No. It wasn't that."

"Then whom did you overhear?"

"It was a talk between Mr. Boddington and Mr. Rowton, in Mr. Boddington's private office this evening."

"You mean that they both know he's innocent?"

"It wasn't said, but I don't see how they could have meant anything else."

"And they said this before you? But you said it was not in the course of your employment?"

"I was standing behind a screen. They didn't know I was there."

"Do you mean it was chance, and they didn't notice you, or were you there on purpose?"

"I hid there to learn the truth."

He controlled his surprise to say: "It was a very brave thing to do. It is more than I should have liked to ask."

"You don't really mean that," she replied steadily. "You mean it's the sort of thing of which you don't suppose anyone to be capable unless they tell you themselves."

"I didn't mean anything of the kind. With the life of that innocent boy at stake, there isn't much I shouldn't approve, if it would get at the truth. I say you did quite rightly, and it was a brave thing to do. Did you get any idea of who really killed Cyril?"

"No. Not the least. And the trouble is I can't remember what I did hear as exactly as I should like. If I'd had the sense to have a note book with me! But I might have rustled a page, if I had, and spoilt it all."

"So you might. I expect you remember what was said sufficiently well, but you'd better have it clear now before the words get more indistinct in your mind. I see how you feel about the way in which you overheard this conversation, especially being in Mr. Boddington's confidential employment, and having access to his room in that way; but you'll remember your promise to me that nothing should be held back that would help in saving Roger Truscott's life. I don't ask you beyond that. Will you tell me, as nearly as you can remember, what was said bearing on that?"

"The trouble is it's so hard to separate."

"Then I think, at any cost of personal feeling, it's your duty to tell me all."

"They were disputing about—other matters, and threatening each other, and Mr. Rowton said Mr. Boddington daren't do what he said he would, because of what happened to Cyril Truscott, and Mr. Boddington replied that he wasn't afraid, because it was a tale that nobody would believe—this is, as against himself. He said that Mr. Rowton would never persuade Menzies to go into the box to swear that he'd perjured himself in the evidence he'd given already, and they wouldn't dare to put the rope round their own necks to injure him."

"And how did it end?"

"Mr. Rowton gave way."

"And is that all you can tell me?"

"Yes. I think it is."

"Miss Morton, you're not being very helpful. Can't you remember the actual words that were used?"

"I can't tell you more than I heard. Mr. Boddington said that the truth was something that no one would believe in a thousand years."

"Did you gather that he had any part in the murder?"

"No. And I don't think he could have had either. I think I could swear from my own knowledge that he wasn't there at the time. Oh, and there was another thing. He talked about the time before the telephone call was put through, and he said he didn't understand it, and didn't suppose he ever should. He wouldn't have said that if he'd been there."

"No. Perhaps not. But he might have shot Cyril and cleared out. What reply did Rowton make?"

"I don't remember that he said anything to that. He just let it pass."

"I've no doubt you're telling me all you heard, but you must admit that it isn't easy to follow. If Mr. Boddington wasn't involved in the murder, and Mr. Rowton and Menzies were—or, at least, are conspiring to perjure themselves in the witness box as to what happened—why should it be a threat against Mr. Boddington? It isn't easy to see that."

"I didn't follow it at all. But that's how it was."

"But Mr. Boddington wasn't frightened by the threats? You said Rowton gave way."

"Yes. So he did. But Mr. Boddington didn't say that he had nothing to fear if the truth were known. He said that they'd never dare tell the truth; and they wouldn't be believed if they did."

Mr. Tonks was reduced to a puzzled silence by the repetition of this statement. It was not one on which he could found any theory of the murder to satisfy his own mind.

"I wish," he said at last, "you'd go home and write down all you can remember of this conversation, whether you show it to me or not."

"Yes. I'll do that. I'm afraid I haven't helped you very much."

"On the contrary, you've made me sure we shall win, though I don't quite see how."

"I don't see how I can go back to Bagley & Co.'s tomorrow."

"Oh, but you must. You might learn the one vital fact on which all depends."

"You're asking a good deal."

"In the cause of justice, and to save the life of an innocent man."

"Well, I'll think it over during the night. I won't promise more."

"And I'm sure you'll have courage to decide in the right way."

CHAPTER XXVII.

LESLIE TONKS spent the next morning puzzling over a problem he could not solve. He felt that, if he could get a theory to fit the facts, he might be halfway toward the discovery of the facts themselves. And it appeared that it was not to be a plausible explanation. It was to be something that no one would believe in a thousand years. That was Mr. Boddington's description, which might not be adequate. He tried to think of fantastic things, but that did not help him at all.

It was midday when Inspector Byfleet phoned him to say that he had found the writer of the anonymous letters. "It's due to you," he said, "to hear what kind of man he is, and the tale he tells, as you put the letters into our hands. I'll tell you, beyond that, that he's no use to us as a witness. I don't think he'll be much to you either, but you may think differently. Anyway, if you care to look in this afternoon, you shall know as much as ourselves."

Leslie thanked him, and arranged to call at Scotland Yard a couple of hours later.

"It's this way," Inspector Byfleet began, when Leslie was smoking comfortably, and had settled himself back to listen. "There's a man on the T. & R. staff named Thornton. Been there as long as Rowton himself, if not more. He has charge of the staff wages, and other disbursements at these London offices, and of a lot of statistical records dealing with the Liverpool works. He said he never saw a Balance Sheet of the firm in his life, and that the work is so distributed that no one except Menzies and Rowton himself knows what's going on, unless it's the Liverpool manager, whom he believes to be in with them. But he says that he'll swear that the business is making a good profit, and always has done. He comes closer to the point when he says that Menzies is in Rowton's pocket, and would swear black was white without winking if he were told to do so. He doesn't say that of Bellman. He says he's always kept a shut mouth, and he knows nothing against him.

"He says he warned Roger at first because he knew there was a plot to rob him of the shares he'd inherited. When he says 'knew,' he ought to say 'guessed,' but that is his own word.

"Now we come to the murder. He says he went out at 1:00 P.M. with the rest of the staff, by the general stairs, but he walked round to the other entrance to get some tobacco at Siskin's shop. He says that Mr. Siskin was standing at the door of the shop, and the assistant served him. The tobacco he bought was in a ready-made packet, and he wasn't in the shop more than a few seconds. As he came out, he saw Roger come through the next door. You'll see that this doesn't leave much time for quarrelling or shooting after the clerks left the office, especially as Thornton says he wasn't by any means the last out.

"He goes further than that. He says that, as Roger came out, he could see inside to the foot of the stairs, and he is certain that there was no dead body there. He says that Roger was quite calm and unhurried, and didn't open or close the door as though he minded anyone looking in."

"Well," Leslie replied, in some surprise that the Inspector should summarise the man's evidence in a way so favourable to the accused, "that's about what I should expect to hear, and it confirms Siskin and Higham in every particular."

"Yes. That's just what it does. But you've got to remember that their evidence has been publicly given, and he knew just what he'd got to confirm.

"And the real snag's here. Thornton hates Rowton and Menzies, and wants to do Truscott a good turn. A few weeks ago, Menzies caught him out in some irregularity in the cash, and reported him to Rowton. Rowton wanted to hand him over to us, but Roger Truscott interceded for him. He doesn't know exactly what happened, but he was whitewashed so that he didn't even have to make good what he was short.

"Now I've given you the facts, and you can call the man if you like. He's not an impartial witness, and he comes a bit late. You won't find him a willing witness either, unless he's sure he's on the winning side. He's in deadly fear of losing his job. Anyway, here's his private address, and it's up to you to do what you like."

Leslie thanked him for this, recognising that he had been very fairly treated, and that the police had been able to make the investigation with a speed and certainty that would have been impossible to his own office, and might not have been equalled by any private enquiry agency he could have employed. He thought that he ought to see the man himself, and judge whether he were telling the truth, in which case he should be called, at whatever cost.

"I think," he added, "the fact that he's an unwilling witness adds to the value of what he says. Gratitude might induce a man to write an anonymous communication that wasn't true, but it would hardly have led him to tell such a tale when you ran him to earth, unless it had really happened. But it's curious how all the evidence stops at the door."

He had spoken with a frankness that responded naturally to the treatment he received. For the moment, they were not experts arrayed on either side of a legal battle, but two men who sought the truth in a difficult problem. But there was a sudden change of manner, not to unfriendliness, but as of a recollected reserve, in the Inspector's answer: "Yes. That's your trouble. Our witnesses were inside when it all happened, and you're picking yours up from the street."

Leslie had an instinctive perception that nothing would be gained by continuing the conversation. He shook hands, and went.

Inspector Byfleet looked after him reflectively. "I wonder," he said to himself. "how much more harm that young man's going to do."

He had been frank about Thornton, feeling that it was due to the defence, as he had had the information from them which had led to him being traced; and, beyond that, he did not think his evidence was of certain value. But he had had other evidence that morning of a different and far more important kind, which he did not intend to communicate to the defence, but which he was following up with a new energy. He meant that the slayer of Cyril Truscott should meet the doom he deserved, and no sentimental considerations would be allowed to deflect him from that resolve.

CHAPTER XXVIII.

IT is not surprising that Diana had a bad night. Excitement is a foe to rest, and indecision can be as potent as fear to the same end.

She had a strong reluctance to returning to the Duckling Street offices. She saw that there might be legitimate differences of opinion as to the duty of an employee who observes criminal practices in those to whom she has sold her loyalty for a weekly reward of seventy shillings. But surely no one could hold it to be an honourable part to remain in such a position and to use it for this purpose of spying upon and betraying those by whom she was paid and trusted. Anyway, it was not a code that would do for her. She decided that Mr. Tonks (naturally putting the interests of his client first) had asked somewhat too much.

Yet reason told her that what she had done was unalterable, and its moral standard would not be raised or lowered by putting her employer to the certain inconvenience that her sudden absence would cause. There was no objection to her returning tomorrow and fulfilling the duties of the day with a normal loyalty. The fact was, she told herself with some self-contempt, it was lack of courage that raised the doubt. It was, at the best, a repugnance to return after what she had done, which was as hard to analyse as to overcome.

Then she considered what her position would be if she should absent herself from her employment without adequate apology or excuse. Such positions were never easy to get. Without references, they might be impossible. She was not entirely dependent on what she earned, but it made the difference between ease and straightened circumstances in the home she shared. Mr. Tonks might help her to another position, but that could be no more than a vague hope; and if she refused to go back now, as he had urged her that it was her duty to do, his sense of obligation might be substantially lessened.

Her mind found no pleasure when it was diverted from this uncertainty to consider some other probable consequences of what she had done. Would she be required to give evidence at the coming trial? Would she have to make public the fact that she had listened behind a screen? She might be praised by those who took Roger's part, but she saw that the incident could be put in another way.

She imagined counsel denouncing her evidence as invented lies. Mr. Boddington would naturally deny it. So would Mr. Rowton. Against the word of those two reputable businessmen they had that of a girl who admitted that she hid in her employer's office, and listened to conversations that were not intended for her! She saw that this publicity, whatever other result it might have, would not enhance her value as a confidential secretary, even to those who might have no criminal secrets to hide.

She imagined her evidence ridiculed, made contemptible, disbelieved. If it were held to be false, it might be that, even for Roger, it would be more potent to harm than help. And at this doubt she forgot herself for a time, thinking of one whose plight was so different from hers, and so much worse that it made her trouble no more than a trivial thing. Suppose what she had done, or could still do, would make the difference to him between condemnation and acquittal, between honour and dishonour, between life and death? And her mind was vexed by a fear that she might have trouble in finding another job! She remembered how their eyes had met in a moment's intimacy that had isolated them in a crowded court. With that memory, she did not feel as one who stakes much in a stranger's cause; she felt she fought for her own.

For most of the major issues of life there are accepted standards of conduct by which people will act without the effort of individual judgement. They judge others in the same way, measuring what they do against a settled standard of law or a social code. It is when a position arises too unusual for common standards to be applied that individual character is most hardly tested, and must rule at the last. From this chaos of thought and feeling, which went on while tomorrow became today, she came to no further decision than that she would not let cowardice hold her back from returning to her employment, and, beyond that, she would leave decision to the events of a later hour.

Having come to the peace which decision brings, she slept so well that she did not wake at the usual hour. Even a shortened breakfast did not enable her to arrive at Duckling Street less than half an hour after Mr. Boddington's arrival, which happened to be earlier than usual; and a few minutes before her appearance, he had made enquiry as to whether she had been unwell the previous afternoon, or said anything about not coming next day.

These questions were negatively answered, and Teddy Watts (meaning no harm on this occasion) added that he knew Miss Morton had been working till late the night before, as he had seen her leaving a few minutes after seven.

Mr. Boddington said: "Oh?" to that, and then: "What were you doing here at that hour?"

"I wasn't here, sir. I was coming along the street."

"And you saw Miss Morton leave?"

"Not exactly, sir. I met her at the corner. I just saw her. We didn't speak."

Mr. Boddington went back to his office without further words. It seemed odd, but there was doubtless some simple, natural explanation. Probably she had just been passing along the street, as Watts had been doing also.

He remembered how his letters had been left ready for signature. He went over to her desk, and inspected her work there. She had left the Sperryn report, as he had instructed her to do. The letters would not have taken more than an hour. Doubtless, she had used his permission to leave early. He was careful that no possibility should be unregarded, as men must be who walk on a slippery edge, but this doubt was too slight and vague to hold him long from the urgent calls of the business day. When she walked in, with apologies for an unpunctuality which was not an ordinary fault, he made no more than a perfunctory answer, and turned at once to the correspondence the morning brought.

During the noon hour, Mr. Rowton came. She was not asked to withdraw, and he said openly that he had brought the £2,000 which he had spoken about investing the night before. He paid it over in notes, and Mr. Boddington had an acknowledgement made out from the usual receipt book. The routine had no suggestion of an illicit payment, and she was shrewd enough to see that this procedure would be strong support for the contention that it was a legitimate and voluntary transaction, arranged between them at the interview which she had herself fixed up on the telephone with an equal openness.

Yet, to her own knowledge, even though her evidence might be disbelieved, the fact remained that it was money paid over reluctantly and on compulsion of a threat that the man who gave it would have been ruined had he refused; that the man who paid it was an embezzler of the funds of the firm he controlled; that the two were engaged in active conspiracy to rob the youthful owners of the major part of the business; and, most sinister of all, that one of those young men had met with a violent death, and the other lay under an accusation of his murder, on which these conspirators had, at least, some knowledge which they would not disclose.

To remain in such an employment would be to condone, if not actually to connive, at the criminality of which she was now wholly aware. Under normal circumstances, this would have been as impossible to her as it would be to remain for the purpose of betraying those she professed to serve. She pondered what she should do now, as she went on with work to which her mind did not give overmuch heed, till her thoughts were sharply interrupted, as the lunch hour approached, by Mr. Boddington's abrupt question: "What time did you leave yesterday, Miss Morton?"

"I didn't look at the time particularly."

"Was it early or late?"

"I didn't notice the time particularly. Why?"

"Teddy Watts said he saw you here after seven."

"Here? That he certainly never did."

"Well, down in the street."

"Yes. I passed him in the street. I remember that. That was in the evening. You said I could leave early yesterday. Should you like me to stay tonight to make up for it?"

Mr. Boddington looked at her for a moment in a silent scrutiny she found it hard to endure. She had lied by implication, if not in explicit words, and she was unsure whether the clumsiness of her answers had betrayed their mendacity.

"I don't think," he said, "that will be necessary. Have you any engagement for lunch today?"

"No," she said; too surprised by the question to give anything but the simple fact.

"Then you shall lunch with me."

The words were an order rather than a request, and left her in doubt, as she followed him down the narrow, winding, ill-lighted stairs, whether he had made a guess at the truth. She could not doubt that she was intended for some further inquisition, and had an impulse of caution, if not of cowardice, urging her to decline the invitation when she should be in the safety of the open street, and leave him there for the last time. But courage conquered, unless it were a less worthy tendency to postpone a crisis she did not like. She stood beside him while he signalled for a passing taxi, and heard his order: "The Falcon Restaurant, Holborn," which announced that he really did intend to give her lunch, rather than to abduct her for immediate murder.

Smiling inwardly, but somewhat nervously, at her own fears (for what warning had Cyril Truscott had of the bullet which sent

him crashing downward to instant death?) she got into the taxi before him, reflecting, as she did so, that though the Falcon Restaurant
may be relied upon for a good meal, and is, in fact, as good (and expensive) a one as those which he frequented regularly; yet her
knowledge of his lunch appointments told her that he was taking her
where it was unlikely that he would be seen by his business associates.

He did not speak during the short ride, but assumed the brood-
ing, introspective expression with which she was familiar when he
would consider a business exploit. It usually meant that a period of
silence would be followed by a curt request that she would get
someone on the telephone, or take down a letter of decisive tone. As
she saw it now, it had implications of ruthlessness, perhaps of menace, which did not arm her with confidence for the coming ordeal.

But his face cleared as their destination was reached, and he
was in his more genial mood as he ordered the lunch, with sufficient
deference to her own choice; nor did he say anything, except on indifferent topics, till the meal was nearing its end.

But then he turned abruptly from a remark concerning the coming tournament for the Wightman Cup, to ask: "Miss Morton, has
Mr. Tonks approached you in any way regarding the Truscott murder?"

With an instinctive wisdom, and forgetting at the moment that
she had made a compact with Leslie Tonks that neither of them
should mention the occasion when he had called upon her, she
armed herself with the apparent frankness of partial truth, to answer:
"Yes, he saw me just after the committal to ask if I knew anything
that could help the defence."

"Where was that?"

"He called on me in the evening at home."

"What made him do that? Why should he think you would be
likely to know anything?"

"He'd seen me taking it down, and thought I must be interested."

"That doesn't sound much of a reason. Anything else?"

"That was the only reason he gave, as far as I recollect."

"What information did you give him?"

"I told him I knew nothing about it. I said"—she lifted her eyes
with a sudden access of confidence as she added this—"that I was
sure that Roger Truscott hadn't shot his brother, but I knew nothing
about it beyond what I had heard in court."

"Do you know more now?"

"No. I wish I did."

"So that was the end of it?"

"I told him I should let him know if I learnt anything that would help to prove Roger Truscott's innocence, as I supposed anyone would, but I'd really nothing to tell. He didn't seem to think my opinion was of much importance, if I'd got no facts to support it."

"He should have approached me in the first instance."

"So I told him."

"If you think young Truscott is innocent, what do you think happened?"

"I've no idea. It's one of the most puzzling cases I ever heard."

"Then isn't it the natural conclusion that the witnesses are right? If you recognise that, you find that there's no mystery left."

"I wouldn't go that far. But I feel sure Roger didn't do it; and I didn't think, when Mr. Rowton was giving his evidence, that he was telling the truth."

"Meaning that he'd done it himself?"

"No. Of course, that's the natural alternative to consider. But somehow, I don't think he had."

"You're a wise girl about that. I don't reckon Rowton knows more about any gun than that the bullet comes out of a hole at one end. And as to shooting Cyril—why, he'd have given a thousand pounds to keep him alive. His death just put all the power into Roger's hands."

"Yes. But if Roger can't get clear of this charge—"

"Then the shares go into some other hands that may be as hostile as he. For the next eighteen months, till he could do his own business his own way, if Rowton had insured Cyril's life for a round sum, I should have said it only showed that he knew where the harbour lay."

He added, as she made no further reply: "Tonks means well, but he's too young for a case of this kind. I had lunch with him yesterday, and gave him a tip that ought to help him over the stile. He'll find counsel takes the same view, unless I'm suffering from senile decay."

"You think he'll be able to prove Roger's not guilty?"

"Oh, I didn't say that. He did it, right enough. But he'll get him off, all the same, if he has the sense to listen to me."

The conversation ended there, and in the taxi returning he only asked if she were feeling comfortable with Ragley & Co., and that in so casual a tone that it might have seemed to be no more than a deliberate making of conversation, when other topics of common interest were not easy to find.

She felt bolder than she had done at first, thinking that the measure of frankness with which she had sustained the inquisition had been successful beyond her hopes. She said: "I'm not popular in the office, though I don't know quite why. Especially not with Mr. Watts, unless I'm making a bad guess. But, being in your own room, that doesn't really matter to me. I'm quite comfortable there.

"You needn't trouble about those young cubs outside, if you suit me. Stick to Bagley & Co., and you'll find you won't have much to regret in the end, if you go on as well as you're doing now."

It was a drawn battle rather than a victory either to her or him. She thought that she had destroyed his suspicions, and that rather by the boldness of truth than by baser methods. She thought (to which she attached some importance) that she had avoided any definite lie.

He was less fully reassured than she supposed. A vague suspicion still vexed his mind, and if he could have destroyed her as easily as he could crush an insect under his thumb, she would not have had many seconds of further life. But that was not so easy to do that it could be considered without more definite cause than he now had.

Short of that, he had shown some adroitness in offering her persuasion of Roger's guilt, linked with the idea that he had himself suggested a way in which he might foil the penalty of the law; and with this the casual hint that she held a position that might be increasingly valuable if her loyalty were assured. And he had said nothing which implied fear on his part, or suspicion of her, or that could have the face of an offered bribe.

Had she been less well-informed already, or less intelligent to understand the values of what she heard, he might not have wasted breath.

CHAPTER XXIX.

IT was during the following morning that Mr. Rowton telephoned to speak to Mr. Boddington, and was informed by his secretary that he would not be in till 12:30. Hearing that, he declined to give any message, and rang off.

At 12:35, he rang again, and Mr. Boddington took the call.

Diana supposed that it was in reference to the new offer of 6s. 3d. a share which she knew to have been received from Lessings' solicitors, with a long argumentative letter to the effect that that was the utmost price that it would be reasonable for them to pay, a copy of which had already been forwarded to Messrs. Tonks & Weatherhead's office.

But the end of the conversation that reached her ears was of a different kind: "Well, what about it? No, of course, not. What do you expect me to do? Well, if you are, I don't see why you're ringing up here. Do you expect me to go out and search the streets?"

A moment later, he rang off without further reply, and with a show of irritation such as he rarely allowed to betray his feelings in business hours. "Blasted fool!" he muttered, as he got up to go out to lunch, but his expression was still perturbed enough to suggest that the information he had received was not as trivial as its reception would indicate.

In fact, Mr. Rowton had rung up to say that Menzies had not come to business that morning. A telephone inquiry had produced the information that he had not been detained by illness. Mrs. Menzies said that he had left, as usual, after breakfast, except that, singularly enough, it had been about half an hour after his customary time. She had connected this with the call of the two gentlemen from the office who had been with him so long the night before. Told that no one had been to see him from the office, she had replied that that was who he had said they were. She was sure he was all right, and declined to be alarmed. (A faint hope that he had been killed by a motor vehicle, and that there would be the insurance money to draw, did flicker across her mind, but she dismissed it promptly as too good to be true.)

Mr. Rowton had telephoned in the rather wild hope that the explanation might lie in Mr. Boddington's office. Mr. Boddington saw the direction of Mr. Rowton's fear, and a concentrated consideration of the problem during a lonely lunch decided him that it was probably of a well-founded quality. Menzies had been persuaded to blab to the police, or to Tonks & Weatherhead, which would be the same thing in the end.

The warning he had received gave him time to consider his own position, which might be extremely difficult. There would be matters for hardy denial, others to be explained away. There would be countermoves to be promptly made. He did not consider the fact that Rowton had warned him, as placing him under any obligation of forbearance in his direction. Rowton had got to sink, if Menzies had split, and if he showed signs of rising to the surface of the cauldron in which he stewed, there would be a pole in Mr. Boddington's own hand to push him under again.

He went back to his office in a very resolute mood, feeling equal to facing anything that the afternoon might bring.

As to that, his time of waiting was short, for he had scarcely settled down to his desk when he was informed that Mr. Tonks and Inspector Byfleet had called to see him.

"Show them in," he said curtly, and rose to greet them with an average measure of affability as they entered the room.

"Could we see you privately?" the Inspector asked, with a glance at Diana.

"There is nothing private from Miss Morton in this office," Mr. Boddington answered. He knew more or less what was likely to be coming now, and it was likely that, if he could satisfy his present callers, he could win Miss Morton's loyalty as a side issue of a quite subordinate but satisfactory kind.

The Inspector looked vexed, but Mr. Tonks said: "I don't think there'll be anything said that Miss Morton shouldn't hear, if Mr. Boddington doesn't object."

Making no further demur, the Inspector opened the subject without preamble.

"The fact is, Mr. Boddington, that we've had a statement made to us this morning which may be quite false—that's likely enough, considering the quarter from which it comes—but we are bound to make enquiries; and, if it is true, it implicates you in the murder of Cyril Truscott in such a way that I'm bound to warn you before I ask any questions that you needn't answer unless you like. But, having done that, it's only fair to give you a chance of explaining anything that you can. You know we only want to get at the truth."

Mr. Boddington took this somewhat startling approach with a quiet gravity. "I'm not entirely surprised," he said, "to hear that there are some developments of this kind, though I didn't think they'd have the nerve to bring my name into it in the way which your warning implies they must have done.

"If I'd anything to hide"—with a slight smile—"I suppose the fairest way would be to ask you to say what the accusations are, and I should know what I'd got to meet; but as it is, you can fire away, and I'll give you all the help that I can. As a matter of fact, it isn't likely that it would have been more than forty-eight hours before I'd be coming round to you—to Mr. Tonks, I mean, not to you, Inspector, in the first instance—though it wouldn't have been about the murder exactly. I'll tell you at once that I don't know more about that than has come out in public, and I doubt whether some of that's true."

"It's the murder we want to talk about," Inspector Byfleet replied, with unsmiling eyes.

"Well, what is it?"

"We are informed that the murder was not only planned, but actually proposed, by you. That you instigated, if you did not actually perpetrate it with your own hand."

"On the face of it, that is absurd. I had no influence over Roger Truscott. To suggest that I should persuade him to murder his brother—"

"It is not suggested that Roger committed the murder."

"Possibly not. I don't recollect where I was that day, but my diary will show, and I expect you can verify it without much difficulty."

"It is not suggested that you were there."

"Then that's one lie the less. Is it Menzies you've got this tale from?"

"Yes, it is...but why should you have supposed that?"

"Because Rowton was phoning this morning. He was in a funk because Menzies hadn't turned up, and at some information he'd got from his wife, and he apparently thought that I'd got hold of the man, and was pumping him here."

"Why should he have thought that?"

"Because he knows that I've been rather disturbed in mind, as the firm's auditor, at some things that have come under my notice recently. I had him here a couple of nights ago, and put it to him straight that if there'd been any concealment of profits in such a way that we had been led to certify balance sheets that showed less than the truth, he'd be a wise man to spit it out frankly now, because I was investigating for ten years past—in fact, ever since the audit was brought to this office—and I shouldn't rest till I knew the truth, let it cost what it might."

There was a subtle plausibility about this reconstruction of the events of the last two days which would have had a convincing quality to Miss Morton's mind, had she not been present at that evening conference and heard a conversation of different kind. As it was, she could only wonder what effect it might have on those who lacked the advantage of that recollection.

Inspector Byfleet did not dispute the adequacy of the explanation, but there was no more geniality than before in the tone of his reply: "Well, it's not a question of accounts. It's a man's death that we're probing now."

"And can you tell me any possible reason I could have for desiring Cyril Truscott's death?"

"No. There seems to have been a little mistake about that. But it was a clever plan, as Menzies tells it, whoever thought of it first."

"I can't discuss that, till I know what the plan was. So far as I understand you at present, the suggestion is that Roger Truscott is innocent, and one or more of those who were on the spot when Cyril was murdered, and who combined to accuse Roger at first, has now turned round to accuse me. It isn't a matter that I can take very seriously, and I rather wonder that you thought it worth putting to me as though I'd got anything to answer carefully. I should have thought you'd have given more attention to those who were on the spot. But if you want to know what underlies it, I reckon it's in this drawer."

As he spoke, Mr. Boddington put his right hand to the top drawer on that side of his desk which was nearer to Miss Morton, and on the further side from that on which his two visitors were seated. Knowing that half at least of what he said was no more than a series of hardy lies, and noticing how closely the Inspector's eyes followed the moving hand, the idea came to her that he looked to see a weapon come from that drawer, such as had shot Cyril Truscott down. It would not have been, to her own mind, an unlikely thing, for she knew that Mr. Boddington kept a gun in one of those drawers, though she could not have said which with certainty.

But, whatever the Inspector thought, he made no motion, and it was nothing more formidable than a sheaf of papers that came out of the drawer.

The Inspector remained silent until they were laid on the desk, his eyes still on the moving hand, until, as it laid them down, the underside of the wrist came into view, and, as it did so, he sprang at the accountant with so fierce and sudden a rush that chair and man fell backward together upon the floor, with Inspector Byfleet upon them.

Diana saw the Inspector's fist come down on her employer's head with what seemed a brutal blow. She saw Mr. Boddington's own fist strike upward at his opponent's chin. She saw him half raised from the floor, with his hand pulling open one of the lower drawers. She heard the Inspector's cry: "Help me, Tonks," and was aware that the two of them were bearing down the desperately struggling man. Her own movement had brought her to the half-opened drawer, from which she snatched a pistol away from the groping hand. The next moment there was a click of handcuffs, and the three men arose in a room that was dim with dust.

"Joe Coghlan," the Inspector said, "I arrest you for conspiracy to murder Roger Truscott, and for complicity in the murder of Cyril Truscott, as its direct result. I warn you that anything you say may be used against you at your trial."

"I tell you you'll regret this, Inspector. I'd no more to do with the boy's death than you had yourself."

"Well, I'll risk that," Inspector Byfleet said easily. "But you know, Joe, it's a mistake that most criminals make. They will try the same dodge twice."

His expression changed to a greater sobriety as he observed that Miss Morton stood with a presumably loaded revolver somewhat casually directed toward his own stomach.

"Miss Morton," he said, with a forced smile, "you seem to have the pull on us all. But would you mind pointing it to the floor?"

A few minutes later the staff of Bagley & Co. had the unusual experience of seeing the head of the firm led through their midst with handcuffs upon his wrists.

CHAPTER XXX.

"IF you really want to know who to thank," Inspector Byfleet said, "you should begin with Miss Morton, and end at the same address."

This was at the dinner that Roger gave at the Royalty on the night of his release to the three to whom he felt that his rescue was due from what might have been no less than a fatal trap.

"Indeed," Diana said, "I did next to nothing. I'm ashamed, now I look back, that I didn't do more. It's Mr. Tonks you should thank first, and then the Inspector, or else the other way round."

"I think, Mr. Truscott, if you'll listen to me," the Inspector insisted, "you will find that I am the better judge, for what I did was no more than my duty—besides that I'd been the one at the first who had run you in—but what Miss Morton did was off her own bat; and why she did it, she's the best one to tell you herself, if you don't know.

Roger's eyes, as he looked at the girl, did not suggest that she was likely to suffer from any lack of gratitude on his part, but he said: "Perhaps if you'd tell me what happened, I should be in a better position to judge."

He knew no more, as yet, than that he had been brought up that morning at the Central Criminal Court, to occupy a seat in the dock while Mr. Wedland-Wedland made a rather mumbled speech, some of which he did not understand, or was unable to hear, at the conclusion of which the presiding judge had said: "Then the prisoner is discharged."

The learned judge had spoken with an impassive gravity, and in a tone as though there were something of which he did not approve, so that it had seemed that he was reluctant to let him go. And then a warder had touched his arm, and he had stepped through the open door of the dock to be led by Mr. Tonks through a hardly-suppressed murmur of applause, to receive the congratulations of a little group that were assembled to welcome him in the corridor of the court, with Mr. Weatherhead at the front; and then to be hurried to a wait-ing taxi at a side door, to avoid the thronging mob that waited his coming out.

Now he looked somewhat pale and worn, but the reaction of feeling, and the resilience of youth, were already combining to re-move the impression of the ordeal from which he came, which was receding already, in these few hours, to the unreality of some dis-tant, fantastic dream.

"Inspector Byfleet," Leslie replied, "is the only one who can tell you what you don't know already."

"We don't often talk about a case that hasn't been heard," the Inspector answered cautiously, "but there are some things, I should say, you've a right to know, after what they were trying to do to you; and I'm not in any fear but that we've got the right bag this time, and shall be able to put them where they belong.

"I won't say that there wasn't a time when I felt the same about you. It does us all good to be wrong sometimes. I wasn't ever satis-fied with the case. I can claim that. I wanted to trace the gun; and I felt that other things were being kept back that I ought to know. But I didn't doubt that you'd shot your brother. I don't see now how I could, with all the evidence that I had. I only felt that we hadn't got all the truth about how it happened, and why. And when I heard that you meant to deny everything, I thought that we never should.

"Even when Mr. Tonks here proved that the telephone call hadn't come through as quick as it should, it only confirmed the idea that there was something outside the murder which was being kept back; and when it looked as though Rowton had been playing a dou-ble game over that contract I thought I smelt what the explanation was. I thought that Rowton would have kept even the murder quiet if he could, not knowing what it might bring out of his own games. I imagined some delay while he debated with Menzies whether they should pin it on to you, as they did, or let a little time go by, and then say that they'd found Cyril shot, but had no idea who could have done it. And I thought that, after ten minutes talk, they had de-cided that the truth was the best card in the pack. Of course, I was miles out, but that's how it looked then.

"But I didn't feel very happy about it, and when I found that Mr. Tonks really believed the defence he was putting up, I deter-mined that there shouldn't be anything left to chance.

"We'd checked up on the witnesses before that, and found noth-ing to make us doubt them. Rowton and Menzies had clean records, and though Bellman had been in trouble once or twice—rather seri-ous trouble—that was before the war, and our instructions are that we're to wink at anything that happened then, if a man's war record was good, and he's gone straight since, as Bellman certainly had.

"We even enquired about Boddington, though he didn't seem to have had a leading part in the piece, and that report was good too. He'd articled himself to Bagley rather late in life, and taken his certificates in time to succeed to the business when the older man died. There were suggestions from more than one quarter that his business methods might not be over-scrupulous, though there was nothing definite, nothing to suggest that he'd be a party to murder, nor could I see any possible motive in that direction. We traced his movements, and were satisfied that he hadn't been anywhere near the scene of the crime.

"Well, you might say we'd done all we could, and more than we need, in a case that was so clear, but I'd made up my mind that I'd try every test I could, and I gave Sergeant Pierce a list of everyone who came into the case, and asked him to give them the once-over, and tell me if he'd ever seen them before.

"Sergeant Pierce isn't very brilliant in other ways, but he's got a memory for facts and faces that you wouldn't easily match. He went through the witnesses, and he said they were all strangers, which, coming from him, was like a good conduct certificate, on the top of the high marks they'd got from us before.

"I didn't dream that anything would come of it, but, just to finish the job neatly, I told him to take a look at the auditor of the firm, whose name seemed to crop up rather frequently, and he came back next day in a state of excitement I'd never seen him show previously. 'Boss,' he said, 'I've seen Joe Coghlan.'

"I couldn't think what he meant at first—the case is fifteen years old, and I wasn't in it at all—but I remembered hearing about it, when he brought it back to my mind.

"Joe was a man who murdered his wife—I oughtn't to say that, because he was tried and acquitted, and he's legally innocent. It was a case where there wasn't room for any half-verdict. It was a brutal, calculated murder, or no murder at all.

"And when it came on for trial, there were three respectable witnesses whose testimony cleared him completely, and left nothing but a very improbable theory of accident to explain how the woman died.

"His counsel was able to show that there had been no opportunity for faking the evidence after the murder. The three witnesses were either telling the truth, or there had been conspiracy between them before the murder occurred, as to how it should be contrived, and what they were each to say. That was too improbable for any

175

jury to bring in a verdict on such a theory, and Joe Coghlan walked out of the dock a free man.

"Twelve months after, one of the witnesses, when he was a dying man, confessed to a neighbour that he had perjured himself, but he was dead before it could be confirmed, or any details obtained.

"The matter was considered at headquarters, and it was decided that nothing more could be done. You can't try a man twice for the same crime. The two witnesses who were still alive might have been prosecuted for perjury, and so might Coghlan himself, but the result wouldn't have been at all sure, and it wasn't clear either that it would be well to give further publicity to what had occurred.

"You see, it demonstrated that any three people can murder another with impunity, if they do it so that they can make a case against a fourth by conspiracy to give false evidence against him. There seems to be no way to get over that.

"Fortunately, it isn't often that three people of such a character will be acting together; and to manufacture false evidence that will endure hostile examination requires more brains than most criminals have ready for use. But the fact remains that it could be done, and it had been done so far that a guilty man had gone free, though, fortunately there had been no innocent one hanged in his place.

"Anyway, as a matter of public policy, it was decided not to stir the mud up again.

"Now here was Pierce saying that Boddington and Coghlan were the same man, and, if that were true, it raised some questions I couldn't leave.

"I went into the records of the two men, and I found that it was a possible thing. Joe Coghlan had disappeared (you couldn't blame him for that) a few months before Boddington articled himself in Bagley & Co's office. That was well enough, but coincidence isn't proof. We'd got photos of Joe still on the file (though I'm not sure that we were in order in that), but he had a hairy face, and Boddington was clean-shaved. And a man changes in fifteen years. We needed something stronger than those photos. And how could Pierce be sure that he recognised a man who had changed so much?

"We'd no fingerprints, for it's the rule to destroy those when a man's acquitted, and there's nothing else on the file against him.

"Still, something had got to be done sharp, and all the more because Mr. Tonks here was getting busy in ways that might give Coghlan warning, if it were he, which was the last thing we wanted, till we had made up our own minds and were ready to strike.

"We'd one mark of identification, if it were still there, a small scar on the inside wrist of the right hand, but a man that we sent to lunch at the next table to him reported that he couldn't see it, and didn't think it was there.

"There was no time to lose, so that night two of us gave Menzies a surprise call. We tried a bluff that came off. We told him the game was up, and he decided we knew so much that his best chance was to offer to fill the gaps, and wriggle out as far as he could in that way. I reckon he's so far right that he's saved his neck from the rope, though he may be an old man when he comes out. We had him at the Yard next morning, and took his statement, and after that we thought it would save trouble all round for him to stay where he was.

"What he told us was this: he said that there was a large sum—a much larger one than any of us may have supposed—at stake in carrying through the sale to Lessings, because the business of Truscott & Rowton had always been prosperous; but for the last ten years large sums had been abstracted annually by Rowton, and put on one side, with the double object of making it appear that the Truscott shares would be of little value when the time would come that you would be able to sell them, and providing means for him to secretly buy a large part of what he intended that you should sell.

"In doing this, he had the help of Menzies and the Liverpool manager, who were to be rewarded with good positions in the reconstructed firm, and a share of the spoils.

"Whether Lessings had any knowledge of the true position of the firm, or how far they may have acted in a legitimate desire to remove competition, and gain the prestige which goes with the older name, is a matter we have not yet had time to consider."

"I think," Leslie interrupted, "you can remove that suspicion from your mind. The bulk of the shares were actually to pass into the control of Rowton and his associates, and the ultimate price was to be settled on the basis of the profits shown during the next three years by Rowton, managing the business as a branch of the larger firm. It was an arrangement which seemed very fair to Lessings' solicitors, eliminating any risk of loss in the amalgamation; and it would, of course have enabled the Rowton gang to reap the full reward of the prosperity which they had concealed."

"Very well, that settles that. It seems that Boddington, who was no fool as an auditor, discovered something of the truth about six years ago, in spite of the elaborate care which the heads of the firm had taken to cover it up. He might have exposed it then, but, instead of that, he insisted on joining the ring. You will probably find that, up to that time, it had been a fraud of a more timid and limited kind, and that it was under Boddington's influence that it had been organised to its present audacity.

"It is probable that all would have gone according to plan, but for your unexpected reluctance to accept the programme. It had been calculated that the influence not only of the head of the firm but of its professional advisers—of whom the solicitors had naturally accepted the accounts certified by Bagley & Co. as genuine documents, and based their decision accordingly—joined to the prospect of so large an amount of cash being offered suddenly for your unrestricted disposal, would be sufficient to induce you to sign the agreement without reluctance; and it was by Boddington's cunning advice that no hint of the firm's (apparent) position was given to you at earlier dates, so that the proposal would be sprung upon you at a time when you would be surrounded by those who would advocate it, and would be without leisure for making investigations or taking independent advice.

"Your unexpected refusal created a position which was the more critical because it was anticipated, and may have been definitely known, that the Brazilian contract would be secured, and was of such a magnitude that it was almost certain to be announced in the press. They saw that, should you have knowledge of that, the last hope would be gone, not merely of your consent, but of your continued confidence in their own integrity. They faced the prospect that their scheme would fail, and the further probability that you would use the power of your vote to expel them from the control of the firm's affairs, with the further risk that this would be followed by discovery of their past irregularities. Indeed, Menzies had a fear that your suspicions had been aroused already, from certain questions you had raised with him.

"The position was therefore desperate, and required an urgent solution, when Mr. Boddington proposed that it should be ended by your assassination, which, he said, could be contrived without risk, if his advice were taken."

"Did you say my assassination?" Roger asked, in a natural surprise.

"Yes. That is where the plan miscarried, somewhat to their own confusion, but also to that of those of us who attempted its investigation.

"According to Boddington's proposal, you were to have been shot, and Cyril charged with the crime. The time and place were naturally to have depended upon opportunity, but substantially he appears to have foreseen that which actually occurred.

"Bellman was to be the actual assassin. Boddington knew him to be a man who would not shrink from any deed of violence, with a promise of safety, and for a sufficient reward. He was also one who could be trusted to keep a shut mouth.

"You may think it a strange coincidence that the man, and his character, should have been known to Boddington, and so opportunely available, but like most coincidences, its singularity disappears when the facts are fully discovered.

"Boddington had known of Bellman from the time of the war, if not earlier. He was familiar with his criminal record, and he had been the means of procuring for him the position with Truscott & Rowton which he now held. His original motive in introducing him to the firm is probably quite irrelevant, and may be beyond discovery, but his knowledge of the man's criminal record both gave him a hold upon him, and was an assurance of his suitability for the part he was now to take.

"When Cyril came to the office that morning in a condition of excitement, and bordering on insobriety, it seemed that they had the opportunity for which they were watching, and Bellman was warned to hold himself in readiness for action immediately that the general office was emptied at the luncheon hour.

"Menzies was instructed to bring a report to Rowton's office at one o'clock, so that he should have a natural reason for being on the spot as a witness.

"Rowton was to have asked the two of you to go with him to lunch, with a suggestion that he had some satisfactory compromise to propose. That would naturally keep you waiting till he was ready to leave. Then, when the offices were otherwise clear, you were to start down the stairs together, and Bellman was to shoot you in the back, which the three of them would afterwards swear to have been Cyril's act.

"In view of his conduct during the morning, and with the three giving the same witness against him, it is evident that he would have had little chance of being believed in saying that one of the others must have done it, even if he could have got any counsel to put forward such a defence.

"The weapon used was to be one which had been in Bellman's possession from the time of the war, of which no one knew but himself—he was not a talkative man—and which it would be impossible to identify, and it was to be left openly on the scene of the crime.

"The plan seemed destined to succeed by its ruthless audacity, as it nearly did.

"Where did it go wrong, at least, so far that the bullet was fired at the wrong man? There appear to have been violent recriminations about this, and a consternation at first which may partly account for the delay which occurred in phoning for the police. But it appears to have arisen about equally from Rowton's over-refinement of detail, Menzies' nervous excitement, and Bellman's stupidity, all joined to the facts that it was a mistake the possibility of which had not been considered beforehand, and that Cyril and yourself, though well-known to Rowton and Menzies, had not become equally familiar to the porter's eyes.

"It appears that Mr. Rowton, hearing the altercation between you, the noise of which penetrated his office partition, and seeing that the hour was actually striking, had delayed to give you the invitation, which would have detained you both. He appears to have thought that you would stay long enough to render that invitation needless and he may have considered that it would be an added security for himself that Cyril would not be able to say afterwards that they were detained by any word from himself.

"When you abruptly decided to go to lunch, and end the discussion, it appears that he heard the movement, and came hurriedly to the door of his own office. Menzies says that he called after you, but you took no notice."

"I don't remember even hearing him."

"Probably not. But Cyril did, and turned back for a few words. Rowton saw that the plan had miscarried, and returned to his own office, probably for no other purpose than to pick up his hat before leaving.

"Menzies, who had been the means of warning Bellman to be in readiness, should have been prompt to observe and to let him know that the plan had gone wrong, but he says that he was not aware that you had left, and admits having given Bellman the final signal that the moment for action had come.

"Cyril paused a moment to wait for Rowton, who came out of his office again, and the two started down the stairs side by side. Bellman, whose account of how he misunderstood Menzies may probably differ somewhat from that gentleman's own explanation, followed them a few paces behind, and shot Cyril as they started down the stairs.

"It is not difficult to imagine the first confusion when it was realised that he had shot the wrong man, nor that it would take a few minutes to consider what all the consequences might be, and what course would be best to take.

"That is the account of your brother's murder, substantially as we have it in Menzies' confession, and I see no reason to doubt that it is substantially true.

"But, as we first considered it, we felt some doubt as to how far it might bring us home. It was the statement of a man who had already sworn in the witness box to a different tale, and it had one feature of suspicion which is almost always present in such confessions, in that it made the part which he had taken in the conspiracy to be somewhat less than that of his fellow criminals.

"It did not follow from that that it was untrue. It is usually those who are conscious of having had no more than a subordinate part in a common crime who may think it more prudent to make confession than to take the full share of responsibility that denial brings. But as an uncorroborated indictment of his companions—and especially of Boddington, who was not on the scene of the murder—it was not evidence of the best quality.

"We decided that the one chance was to interview Boddington, and, if possible, surprise and confuse him into such admissions as would enable us both to confirm the truth of the tale we had, and to present it in such form as the law requires.

"As Miss Morton knows, we did not find him an easy victim, and I do not say that he might not have bluffed his way through successfully even then, if I had not observed the little scar on his wrist which gave certainty to my mind that we had the man before us in whose brain your brother's murder had first been schemed, and warned me, at the same time, that he was likely to prove a desperate and resourceful criminal, who should be allowed no warning of what I knew.

"It is an illustration of that curious tendency by which the criminal does so much to simplify the problem of his own detection: the tendency to repeat himself.

"We learn to build with certainty on the presumption that the criminal who has escaped by some particular form of duplicity will try the same again in his next emergency, although its repetition may be reasonably calculated to expose its falsehood. The poisoner will not use the knife; and the writer of begging-letters seldom makes an effort to bilk his landlady. Even the burglar who is accustomed to enter by the side window will rarely use the back door.

"So that's the tale, Mr. Truscott; and if you say you've got cause to thank me, I should say you're wrong. It was the way that Mr. Tonks took up your cause that made me feel that it needed a second look, and whatever some people may think or say, we never want to fix a crime on the wrong man."

"I do thank you, all the same," Roger answered, looking at Diana the while he spoke, so that the gratitude of his eyes was hers, whatever his lips might say; though the justice of this may deserve more than a moment's doubt. "But there's one thing that puzzles me. I understand that Boddington or Joe Coghlan, or whoever he really is, is to be charged with Cyril's murder, and I should have thought that, even on Menzies' statement, he's clear of that, for he never meant to kill Cyril, whatever he meant for me."

"Not meant to kill you!" Diana said, "I should say that he meant to kill you both, and the second was the worse way."

"There is a good deal of force in Miss Morton's argument," Leslie agreed, "but I don't think the law will need to go quite so far. When men combine for some felonious end, and the death of an innocent man is the first consequence, the law regards them as sharing a common guilt, and knows how to call it by the right name."

It was an opinion with which Inspector Byfleet agreed. "You'll find they'll put up a good fight, and the lawyers' pockets will be a bit fuller before it's done, but that won't make any difference to how it ends. It'll mean that the hangman will earn three fees on one day, which is more luck than he often has.

"But you don't need to think about that. You need a good holiday before you come back to take control of your father's firm, and Miss Morton looks to be needing one of about the same length and from the way you used to gaze at her during those two days in the dock, when most men would have had other things on their minds, I should say that a little matrimony would do you good."

ABOUT THE AUTHOR

SYDNEY FOWLER WRIGHT (1874-1965) penned over seventy volumes of science fiction, fantasy, classic mysteries, historical novels, poetry, and non-fiction, many of them being published by the Borgo Press Imprint of Wildside Press.